WHEN YOU ARE MINE

IRIS T CANNON

Copyright © 2023 IRIS T CANNON

All rights reserved

The characters and events portrayed in this book are fictitious. Any similarity to real persons, living or dead, is coincidental and not intended by the author.

No part of this book may be reproduced, or stored in a retrieval system, or transmitted in any form or by any means, electronic, mechanical, photocopying, recording, or otherwise, without express written permission of the publisher.

ISBN-13: 9798320058047

CONTENTS

Title Page
Copyright
CHAPTER 1   2
CHAPTER 2   7
CHAPTER 3   13
CHAPTER 4   19
CHAPTER 5   23
CHAPTER 6   28
CHAPTER 7   31
CHAPTER 8   39
CHAPTER 9   45
CHAPTER 10   51
CHAPTER 11   57
CHAPTER 12   61
CHAPTER 13   66
CHAPTER 14   73

CHAPTER 15	79
CHAPTER 16	84
CHAPTER 17	91
CHAPTER 18	97
CHAPTER 19	103
CHAPTER 20	108
CHAPTER 21	113
CHAPTER 22	119
CHAPTER 23	129
CHAPTER 24	134
CHAPTER 25	139
CHAPTER 26	144
CHAPTER 27	151
CHAPTER 28	157
CHAPTER 29	162
CHAPTER 30	167
CHAPTER 31	178
CHAPTER 32	183
CHAPTER 33	188
CHAPTER 34	193
CHAPTER 35	198
CHAPTER 36	203
CHAPTER 37	209
CHAPTER 38	215

CHAPTER 39	220
CHAPTER 40	225
CHAPTER 41	231
CHAPTER 42	236
CHAPTER 43	241
CHAPTER 44	246
CHAPTER 45	251
CHAPTER 46	256
CHAPTER 47	261
CHAPTER 48	266
CHAPTER 49	272
CHAPTER 50	277
CHAPTER 51	282
CHAPTER 52	287
CHAPTER 53	292
CHAPTER 54	297
ALSO BY THE AUTHOR	323

WHEN YOU ARE MINE
By Iris T Cannon
Copyright © 2023 Iris T Cannon

CONTENT WARNINGS

This book contains subject matter which may be distressing to some readers. Themes include rape &/or sexual assault, stalking, kidnapping, sex scenes, murder and violence.

CHAPTER 1

OLIVIA

My feet hit the pavement hard as I run through Central Park. The paths are littered with people and I meander through the crowds, trying hard to avoid hitting anyone. There is a gnawing pain in the pit of my stomach that I just can't shake off. My mind is a jumbled mess, my cluttered thoughts distracting me from concentrating on anything other than the disaster that was last night.

When my phone vibrates, I tap my earpiece and slow to a brisk stroll as I answer. It's Amy; solid, dependable Amy who has been my best friend since that first day in Kindergarten all those years ago. She's also the person who I can't imagine not being in my life. We've gone to school together, then on to college, and now work in the same company. She's my lifetime companion, the one thing I insisted on when taking on this position for Ainsley Winmore, who's known us both since we were literally in diapers.

"How's the bride-to-be this morning?"

Amy's voice is laced with humor and I know

she's dying to laugh, but she needs to tread carefully. I don't know anyone else who can quite pull off simultaneously making me laugh and making me want to cry as well as she does. She's my oldest friend, and I love her to death, but today she could very easily become a homicide victim. My homicide victim.

"On a scale of one to ten, how bad is it?" I ask her. I only saw the one paper this morning, but Amy's an early riser—I know she already would've surfed every social media outlet on the planet and then some.

"On a scale of one to ten, I'd say you're edging dangerously close to a twenty. Your engagement is all anyone is talking about."

"So if I refute the engagement, I'm going to go down in the history books as the evil witch that broke Thomas Thackeray's heart."

"Did you honestly not see that one coming?" Amy asks me.

"I knew it was coming, Ames. Just not the way he did it. It's too much too soon."

"My suggestion is you roll with the punches and pray for a miracle. Your father can't afford any bad publicity right now."

I roll my eyes and exhale the huge sigh I didn't know I'd been holding in. I know my father would be in a bad position if I were to disregard my engagement. He is still reeling from an investigation into his business dealings, in which he was accused of questionable practices in order to win some of the city's largest construction contracts. I couldn't bring any more unwanted attention to him.

"Tell me there's light at the end of the tunnel," I plead, coming to a stop on a grassy knoll and turning in a semi-circle like I've lost my balance. This was too much. I was sure I would lose my mind soon just thinking about how my life had literally changed overnight.

"Give it a few days; I'm sure people will find something else to talk about."

I hang up and look down at my phone. When I think about the train wreck that's coming, I want to throw the damn thing into a pool of water and pretend like it doesn't exist. My introverted self just won't be able to deal with all the pressure squeezing me into the spotlight.

I shake my limbs out and regain my momentum, getting back onto the concrete path. I enter too quickly, so engrossed in my own thoughts that I don't watch for traffic. I end up getting sideswiped by a bike messenger who sends me hurtling to the ground, where I land on all fours, grazing my knees.

"Mother..." I curse, but before I can finish, strong arms are pulling me up from behind. I'm so off balance I manage to stumble into a concrete wall before I can right myself again.

"You okay?"

I pull myself away from the person and turn at the sound of his deep voice. I find myself staring up into the face of a stranger. He's tall and firm, his hard body rippling with muscle beneath his suit. I realize he was the concrete wall I stumbled into.

"I'm fine," I mutter, wiping my palms against my pants. They sting like a bitch and I can feel the cuts where the gravel has peeled back my skin. This was all I needed to complete such a fine morning.

"You sure? That's a mean tumble you took there."

I look at the man in the suit, and I have to crane my neck slightly to see his face. Boy, is he huge. And not in a bad way. His height puts him at a head taller than me, and his designer shirt stretches across his chest, defining the strength hidden beneath. Everything about him reeks of money and power. I come from both, yet still I'm intimidated by him.

"You sure you're not concussed?" He frowns at me like he's waiting for me to say something. "You zoned out there for a minute." Or maybe not.

"I'm fine," I assure him, reaching back to let my messy ponytail out before I re-tie it. I can feel the loose tendrils as they lash at my face.

He has his phone out, and he's looking down at it. Once again, I blank out as I look at his face, taking in every minute detail. Which is so not like me. I don't think I've so much as looked at another man since Thomas and I started dating two years ago.

The stranger angles his body away from me, giving me a side profile of his perfectly chiseled cheeks. He occupies himself with something on his phone but doesn't walk away. His 5-o'clock shadow looks like it has found its permanent residence along his jaw, his eyes a mesmerizing blue against his thick brown hair folded back on his head in luxurious waves. It should be criminal for a man to look so perfect.

"I'm fine. Really. Thank you. I'm fine."

I start to walk away from him backwards, continuing on my route as he looks up and maintains eye contact with me.

"Give me your number," he says, as I retreat. This guy is unbelievable. I laugh and shake my head, taking off in a soft sprint in the opposite direction.

CHAPTER 2

JACK

I never walk through Central Park. And when I say never, I mean never. It was purely by chance that I happened to be there to help the damsel in distress that was knocked over by some asshole bike messenger who didn't even stop to see if she was all right. For some inexplicable reason, I'd asked Willis to stop the town car at the mouth of the park as we headed to my appointment and told him I'd cut through the park on foot. Even Willis, knowing me for the creature of habit I am, balked at the thought of me doing such a thing.

And so I'd found myself walking past at the precise moment that the girl was knocked over and fell on all fours in front of me. And when I helped her up, it was all I could do to stop myself from doing something foolish as I watched her and listened to her tell me that she was fine. She looked fine. She looked damn fine. With legs that went on forever in her tights, and caramel colored hair with blonde highlights that dazzled like diamonds in the sun. Her blue eyes were twin orbs of ice—a mesmerizing cerulean with fathomless depths.

And then when my damn phone had chirped, forcing my eyes away from her, she'd picked herself up and fled without a backward glance at me, refusing me further contact. Of course, I knew who she was. I knew exactly who she was. How could I not when she was left right and center of every story on my news feed? She was hard to miss. And I didn't think there was a person in the world right now that wasn't aware who Olivia Kane was after the announcement of her engagement to Thomas Thackeray went viral last night.

◆ ◆ ◆

"Jack, thank you for re-arranging your schedule to meet with me so this early this morning."

"I've learnt to make concessions when I'm dealing with the best in the business."

I smile and kiss Ainsley's forehead in greeting.

We make small talk, updating each other on work and aspects of our unfolding lives. I fall comfortably into conversation with Ainsley, a formidable businesswoman who holds interests in all facets of the construction industry.

"I heard about your acquisition of JLH Group," she says, raising her eyebrows in appreciation. "I never thought I'd see the day that John Limon would sell his chain."

"Let's just say, between friends, he wasn't too happy about selling. Especially to me. But his vices got the better of him."

"I'm aware the man has been snorting his business into the ground."

"His loss, my gain," I tell her.

"What are your plans for the hotels?" she asks me.

"Overhaul. Redecorate.Rebrand. It's a profitable line if one knows what they're doing."

"And you're certainly doing well for yourself," she muses.

I give her a small smile. She must have read about my entry into the '40 Richest Under 40'. I'd made it onto the list last month as I scraped past my first billion dollars in net worth. What the world didn't know was that was just the tip of the iceberg. If I'd had my way, I'd have stayed off that list permanently, opting instead for a life not well documented. I appreciated my privacy above all else. Publicity like this didn't do much for me past my public image. Oh, and all the gold-diggers that came knocking on my door.

"The reason I wanted to meet so early, as I explained over the phone, is because I have a flight in two hours. I'm afraid I won't be able to attend the club tomorrow as agreed, but I do have the preliminaries here."

Ainsley rolls out her sketches on the table.

I make no move towards them. I have always dealt with Ainsley and only Ainsley for any and all interior design work I have. She is my go-to person. I don't want to use anybody else, and yet, I'm not willing to lose her altogether. I have to hear what she has to say, if for no other reason other than as a courtesy to her.

"I can't afford to push the opening back, Ainsley."

I give the older woman a pointed look. I'd worked with her on several projects over the past seven years; her eye for design was second to none, which is why I kept coming back to her time and time again. The thought of working with anyone else was giving me anxiety and causing a rod of nervous heat to creep up my spine.

"I'm not asking you to," she explains. "I have a designer I've mentored myself. She's as thorough —if not more so—than I am. I think you'll find she's a good fit."

"And if she's not?"

Even to my own ears, it sounded like a threat, even though there was no way I could ever threaten Ainsley. Truth be told, she didn't need my business; she was a made woman even before I started with her. There was therefore no point in making vague references to what might or might not happen in her absence.

"I guarantee you this designer will deliver you a club beyond your expectations, and in the timeframe specified. And if she fails to do so, the work and furnishings acquired are on the house."

This is what I like about Ainsley. Knowing that she's not in a relationship for financial gain. She appreciates my friendship enough to put her trust and faith in someone that she knows would not let me down. I can't fault her for that. And I can't refuse a request she makes when I know her judgement is sound and beyond reproach.

◆ ◆ ◆

I leave Ainsley's office with a promise for her to do a walk through once she's back from her trip. I'm willing to take a chance on her recommendation—one of her many minions—and I have no doubt she's sending me the best. I've just settled into the town car when my phone rings and Selena informs me she's received the brief from Ainsley and organized a meeting with her candidate for the next morning. I'm running on fumes as I consider all the things that could go wrong with this new designer.

But then I push all thoughts of the meeting to the back of my mind and turn my attention to thoughts of the girl I ran into in Central Park earlier. I find myself watching the area as we drive past, my eyes alert for any sign of her, knowing the likelihood of ever seeing her again is near improbable. And even if I did see her again, what of her fiancé? I surprise even myself with these thoughts. I'm never taken with a woman. I rarely come across one who I afford a second thought, so I'm surprised that I find myself replaying the morning's events in my head over and over again.

"You have the lousiest timing, Jack," I mutter to myself, wondering why today of all days I had decided to walk through the park and run into someone as unattainable as happiness itself.

CHAPTER 3

OLIVIA

What most people don't know is that my training in interior design started way before my entry to College. Ainsley Winmore is my Godmother. So while other kids were busy growing up from infancy to adulthood, I was already on my way to being groomed into the person I am today. A lot of what she's taught me has shaped me into today's version of Olivia Kane.

Ainsley has lived a semi-reclusive life—granting only select interviews over the years. She shies away from the media, even when she is constantly making headlines with her latest success story or the empire she's quietly built herself. Her deep need for privacy has rubbed off on me in such a way, I could be considered the oddity in today's society for my lack of social media presence. Which is exactly why I almost lose my shit when Thomas announces our 'engagement' to the world without prior consent, knowledge, or even agreement from me. Although we'd touched on the subject briefly and informally—all roads lead to here sort of stuff—

we'd never actually had a formal discussion about it, and I'd believed the matter had been put to bed. I mean, I'm twenty-four years old—what's the rush, anyway?

So, when Thomas blindsides me in front of the whole world, knowing there's nothing I can do but grin and bear it and flow with the tide, it's all I can do not to curl up in a ball and hide from the flash of the cameras stuffed up in my face at the charity ball last night. His announcement was as much a surprise to the world as it was to me. Although, I have to say, the world loves a great love story and welcomed the news. While I did not.

Ainsley is literally one of the only people on this earth who can understand me just by reading my facial expressions. She knows my moods and my weaknesses and has always been there in the background to help me back up whenever I fall. She purses her lips and cuts a formidable image as she stands behind her desk with her white knuckles folded onto the rich oak top.

She's never liked Thomas. She made that clear the first time I brought him home to meet her and my father. Ainsley has a deep mistrust of people, and an uncanny ability to read situations beyond what the naked eye can see. Even before he put two sentences together, she had already made up her mind about him and told me that I was destined for bigger things. My father had been indifferent—polite and courteous, but not wrapped in the boy I'd brought home the way I imagined most fathers usually are. Which was odd, because Thomas Thackeray was all the things a father could possibly want for his daughter. He was young, handsome, successful, and came from a family who had belonged to the upper echelons of society for hundreds of years. He worked in finance and had an impressive portfolio. Oh, and he was that eligible bachelor that was followed around the city by overzealous yuppie types, groupies and paparazzi.

"I know you're not happy about this," Ainsley says, throwing a newspaper across the desk at me. She's never had occasion to berate me, but her voice is scathing as she addresses me. "The images of you say it all."

I shrug, telling her there's not much I can do about it. The surprise on my face the minute Thomas made the announcement was captured in high definition on every camera in the room then plastered all over every media platform in existence. I looked ridiculously like a deer caught in headlights.

"Did you know he was going to do this?"

Ainsley loves that I've grown to be like her and shunned the media. She's always believed that the press is a vehicle for disaster. That's why she's gone out of her way to avoid them like the plague. She also believes that an air of mystery adds credibility to a person's character.

"No, I didn't."

"So why didn't you refute the engagement then and there? Why did you go along with his preposterous charade?"

I can see she has the same concerns as I do. A broken engagement is going to bring bad press to my father. It's going to paint me in a bad light —the Thackerays are the Saints of Society—and the longer this charade goes on, the harder it's going to be for me to extricate myself from this engagement.

"You know how awkward I feel in front of the camera," I remind her. "He really did take me by surprise."

Ainsley folds her arms against her chest. She reminds me of a defiant teenager trying to get her way. Her silvery blonde hair is pushed away from her face into a loose chignon, the way she's always worn it. I stare at her cheekbones, cut severely high, her Slavic heritage never more apparent than it is now with the curse of a scowl across her lips. She's in her early fifties and she's a force to be reckoned with, especially when she's on the warpath. Which is now.

"Let me ask you something, Olivia." She pauses, unfolds her arms and looks down at a spot on the desk before she takes a deep breath. She wants to ask, but she's afraid of the answer, and I know this from the nervous chortle of her breath as she inhales. "Do you want to marry Thomas?"

"It's not a matter of whether or not I want to marry him, Ainsley. We've been together for more than two years—marriage is the obvious next step in the equation."

She looks at me thoughtfully, her assessing gaze probing into my soul. This is how she always got to the heart of me. "You didn't answer the question."

My silence is probably the thing that's going to seal this deal for her. She gives me a knowing gaze then a short nod, as though I've told her everything she needs to know. The press of her lips is firmer as she quietly takes a seat and shuffles some papers around her desk. She's usually so orderly, but I can see today I've ruffled some feathers. She may be my Godmother, but she's been more like a mother to me throughout my life after I lost my mother when I was four. They were best friends, and Ainsley has kept a watchful eye over me and my father since the loss. She was never more than a stone's throw away from us, even throughout her three marriages.

"I have to take a business trip," she tells me, not looking up. "I trust you can manage without me for a few days."

"You've taught me well."

"There's also a project I need you to handle. It needs to get under way as soon as possible. The company's PA will call this afternoon and set a meeting with you."

I frown. "What about the Bowen project?" That job is taking up all my energy, and I'm not sure taking on another big project simultaneously is feasible.

"This new project is the priority," she tells me. "For personal reasons, I can't have this account walk."

CHAPTER 4

JACK

Selena is on her phone talking in an animated way about the wedding of the century. Generally, such subjects don't interest me, simply because I'll never be getting married. Ball and chain, definitely not for me. But it's when I walk past her as she's chatting away in the conference hall that I come to a complete stop at the mention of Olivia K. I backtrack until I'm standing almost at the doorway, listening to a one-way conversation about a woman I'm almost sure I conjured up in my head.

I can't believe I'm doing this. I'm eavesdropping on a conversation, something I've never done before. And I've never given much thought to wanting to know anything past the basics about a person. The sudden interest I have in this stranger I met briefly is surprising even me.

I listen intently, getting what I believe is the tail end of the conversation, and I hear Selena literally fawning over a dress that Olivia was wearing at a gala last night. Apparently the dress was sold out in stores by mid-morning today and has now been labelled the Olivia K.

She has a dress in her name.

The public have named a dress after her.

The designer of that dress is probably working around the clock to get more of that dress into the hands of hungry consumers.

These are the things I'm thinking when I come back down to earth with a heavy thump when Selena waves her hand in front of my face, trying to snap me out of my thoughts.

"Sorry Jack, I didn't see you standing there waiting. Did you need something?"

"I didn't want to interrupt your call," I tell her.

"Don't worry about it. Just Ivy gushing about running into a celebrity last night."

"Oh? Who?"

Selena gives me a comical look. She knows I'm not usually curious about such things, and definitely not about celebrities. If anything, I steer very well clear of any sort of publicity when I can avoid it, so my interest has definitely got her asking questions.

"Didn't think you were interested in the gossip columns," she muttered.

"It's not gossip if she actually met the celebrity, right?"

"What's going on with you?" she asks me. The look on her face tells me she thinks I've gone a little weird. I decide to feign ignorance and get back to basics.

"I was looking for the Stratton file," I tell her. "I was sure I left it on my desk."

"I have it right here," she says, as I come to her desk. She grabs the file and hands it to me. "I was scanning the documents to the server."

"Appointments?"

"The Workshop cancelled this afternoon's appointment."

I look up at Selena and frown, giving her a look of disbelief. "Again?" Ainsley Winmore had assured me there would be no hiccups with her design team in her absence. It had been hard enough getting an appointment in the first place, and now they were cancelling a second appointment? If it weren't for my history with the woman, I'd have already gone elsewhere.

"Sorry, boss. Do you want me to call someone else?"

I shake my head in irritation. "No, call them back and get a commitment. I don't care how you do it, just make it happen. This project needs to get off the ground now."

◆ ◆ ◆

When I'm in the confines of my own office, I pull up the website of the charity that ran last night's gala. I can't help myself. I have to see what all the fuss is about. I go through an endless reel of photos until my eyes land on a couple of photos of Olivia in a dazzling emerald green dress that boasts a split up the length of one calf. Her hair is swept up in an unruly mess that makes her look like a million dollars. Her makeup is subtle, natural shades on a natural beauty, her smile the kind that obviously breaks hearts. She is luminous and breathtaking as she captivates the whole room. Her fiancé is standing beside her but has his head turned away. She has her head craned to the right as she engages a group of people in conversation. I find myself scanning the faces of the people surrounding her; even those not in her close proximity are watching her in reverence, much in the same way I imagine they would watch a queen approaching. It's not hard to see that Olivia Kane commands a room when she enters it. She is the people's royalty, and they love her.

I shut the computer and turn in my chair to face the window. I always turn to nature when I need to think with a clear head. I don't know, don't understand really, why this woman has such a hold on me. I have not stopped thinking about her since I ran into her a few days ago in Central Park. Even things that usually irritate me haven't so much as raised a spark out of me for all the time I've spent consumed with thoughts of her. It's just not right that she's come out of nowhere, blitzed my life like a hurricane, and left such an indelible mark on my life.

CHAPTER 5

OLIVIA

As soon as my ass hits the chair, Amy buzzes me on the intercom and advises me my next meeting should be arriving in 15 minutes. I've just put the phone down when she pokes her arm through my door, luring me with a fresh cup of coffee.

"Come in," I laugh. "I promise I won't bite."

"How's the blushing bride-to-be?"

She bats here eyelids and narrowly misses my pen as it goes flying toward her head.

"Tell me this year will be over eventually," I mumble.

"You can talk to me about anything, you know that, right?" she reminds me, throwing me a sympathetic look. Amy's never liked Thomas, either. She's always believed I deserved much better.

"Now, Amy," I remind her "that's what therapy is for. You are my person when I need a pick me up or a good time. I'm fine, really. I know you're worried, but there's really no need to be. We were headed down that road, anyway."

She gives me a disbelieving look before she throws out, "Though a little premature, don't you think?"

I shrug. Sooner or later, Thomas and I would have gotten engaged. It was a given. The organic next step.

I look at Amy. Beautiful, dependable Amy with her loyal heart and larger than life soul. In a life of so much mayhem, I owe her my sanity for always being by my side. I smile softly as she diverts the conversation to work, knowing my personal life has run out of steam. She runs through updates on all our outstanding projects, bringing me up to speed. She tends to be animated when she speaks, and her blonde hair bobs with her as she uses her whole body to convey various messages. Her stormy grey eyes are fixed on me when she tells me about my next meeting.

"I'll walk you through the final sketches later this afternoon after you've cleared your meetings. Speaking of which, the representative from GABLE should be here soon."

"Remind me who that is again?" I say, frowning. "I don't recall the name."

"It's the portfolio that Ainsley organized before she left. The meeting you cancelled last week?" She lifts her eyebrows at me in question, silently asking if I'm really okay. I can't have already forgotten about Ainsley's meeting. "He insists on meeting you today; if this meeting doesn't happen today, I'm sure he'll walk."

"Oh fuck. I did miss that meeting, didn't I?"

"Yes. Twice."

I scrub my hand down my face in agitation and curse the moment I let Thomas take control of my life. He's thrown me off my game. I like everything nice and neat and orderly. Planned down to the last dot. Surprises that catch me off guard quite literally throw me into a tailspin, which is exactly what Thomas's engagement announcement has done to me. It has resulted in me taking a few days off work just to gather my thoughts and recover mentally.

"I've been fielding calls from them daily. I understand why Ainsley doesn't want to lose this contract. They're big on the East Coast and on the international front. I believe they've just started taking a more active role on the West Coast. This company is huge."

"I think it's more personal for Ainsley than that," I mutter, turning to the window. "Let me know when he gets here."

Amy clacks away on her low-heeled sling back pumps. I watch her walking away and thank the Lord, yet again, for giving her to me. I honestly don't know what I'd do without her. She is my best friend, my right hand, and also my personal assistant, forgoing a career in public relations to work alongside me.

A few minutes later, she pops her head around

the corner of my door and, with some excitement, announces the arrival of the GABLE rep. I shuffle some papers on my desk, setting them aside and rise in greeting, holding out my hand in welcome to...

The stranger in the park. I feel my lips move, but nothing escapes as I look from the newcomer to Amy, then back again, allowing my hand to sit within the firm grip of the man standing in front of me. For a moment, I take in his looming presence and the impeccably tailored suit he wears. It's definitely the man I ran into in Central Park last week. I'd know that amazing face anywhere.

"Jack Speed," he announces, before Amy, who stands gaping at me can find her footing and introduce us.

"Olivia Kane," I reply, indicating the seat in front of me. I look at Amy and give her a smile, but she doesn't budge, following the movements of my visitor as he unfastens the button of his jacket and takes a seat in front of me. I notice his thighs are built like a footballer's and have to stop myself from drooling.

"Amy?" She snaps out of her trance and smiles awkwardly before walking to the door and announcing she'd be right outside if I need anything. She closes the door behind her; that in itself tells me she is still dazed, as I never close my door. Ever since I've been young, I've always insisted on open doors. Even my office door was always open and my space welcoming to everyone who needed me.

"We met in Central Park, correct?"

"I'm glad you remember," he says, crossing a long leg over one knee.

"You've changed your day job?" I ask. "No longer rescuing damsels in distress in the park?"

He throws his head back and chuckles deeply, and I can feel his humor as it fills the room. "Beautiful and funny," he exclaims. "Apparently, this meeting was supposed to happen last week, but it got delayed because the head designer was unavailable. More than once."

I take the words for what they are—a jab at last week's cancellations, which he obviously isn't happy about. If his tone and arrogant smirk are anything to go by, he's definitely not impressed.

"Well, it's happening now," I smile, but I have sudden misgivings about meeting with this pompous ass.

"Finally," he breathes, looking out the floor to ceiling window at the skyline beyond. I look at him in profile and notice the chisel in his cheekbones, a severe cut that's covered in whiskers. "Finally, you've made time for me."

CHAPTER 6

JACK

"I think we've gotten off on the wrong foot," she says, as I look toward the window and continue to ignore her. Of all the things I was expecting, this was definitely not one of them. By some cosmic alignment of the stars and the sun and the moon, Olivia Kane and I cross paths again.

My initial conviction stands. I will not get involved with a woman who already belongs to someone else. I will, however, bask in this feeling of fullness I have in her presence. With her, I feel like I'm home. I have no idea how long she's worked for Ainsley, but I find it hard to believe that we have never had occasion to meet before since we are both closely related by a mutual contact.

Given she is all I've thought about for the past week, I'm not sure why I do it, but I decide to be a total dick toward her. I casually ignore her presence, even as she works hard to please me. She's apologized a few times now for flaking on our appointments, and I know she's sincere, but I still can't help but give her a hard time about it.

I finally turn my eyes to look at her, saying nothing, then rise from my chair, button my jacket, and walk quietly over to the window, looking down at everything New York City has to offer. I continue to ignore her, as though she's said nothing, and don't even acknowledge or accept her apology. Instead, I keep her sitting on the edge of her chair as frustration replaces her quiet patience.

"Is there a problem?" she asks, after several minutes of interminable silence.

"You can see Central Park from here," I mutter, more to myself. "How do you ever get any work done with a view like this?" I turn to look at her suddenly, inquisitive. I can see by the look on her face that my words have insulted her.

"I can assure you," she says, smarting at my implication, "I get all my work done. On time. Every time."

I turn my head back to the window, but not before she sees the arrogant smirk that breaks out on his face.

"I'm sorry, how did you say you know Ainsley Winmore?" she asks, her curiosity getting the better of her.

"I didn't."

She lets out an exasperated sigh, closing her eyes momentarily before she takes a deep breath. Her patience is quickly evaporating.

"Let's get this meeting underway, shall we?" She suggests this in a way that tells me she's trying to assert some authority and take control of the conversation. But she's failing miserably.

"It is underway. What would you like to discuss?"

"We can't very well discuss this project with you standing at the window."

"So come join me."

I give her a cheeky grin. On any other day, she may have found my playfulness charming, but she looks right now as though she is about to throttle me.

"Look, Jack, it looks like for some reason, you don't want to be here. We'll contact GABLE and have them send over another rep if that serves your needs better. Call it collaborative differences."

The grin falls from my face and is quickly replaced with a stony mask. My hands are burrowed deep in the pockets of my pants. I can feel a tight muscle in my temple as it flickers. I hold my tongue until I can hold it no more. When I finally speak, I don't say what she wants to hear.

"You do that," I tell her, walking toward the door. She makes no move to stop me. Instead, she watches as I walk out of the office without a backward glance.

CHAPTER 7

OLIVIA

The minute he is gone, I buzz Amy and she comes scurrying into my office. "Oh my God, what happened?" she asks, a horrified look on her face. "That was the shortest meeting in the history of time."

"Get GABLE on the line and ask them to send over another rep."

"Olivia, what happened? What did he do?"

"Nothing. Precisely nothing. That asswipe was more interested in the view than getting any work done," I fume. "Get them to send us someone that actually wants to be here."

A few moments later, Amy rushes back into my office, her face ashen, clutching a pen that she flicks on and off intermittently. Oh no, I warn myself. I know that tic. It means she's nervous.

"What is it?"

"GABLE. They can't send anyone else."

"Well, why the hell not?" I am irritated more than anything else. What sort of an outfit was I dealing with here?

"Because this morning you met with GABLE's

CEO."

♦ ♦ ♦

Amy has to grovel to get back into GABLE's graces and arrange this meeting. One which I'm told his PA, Selena was very reluctant to set. But I somehow have to smooth over GABLE and get them back on board with this project—otherwise Ainsley will kill me, and I don't think I'm quite ready to die yet. I'm not sure who I'll be meeting with, but I'm assuming it won't be Jack Speed, which is little consolation, but it's something.

I walk up a flight of stairs, through dark hallways behind a security guard who shows me to 'the boss's office'. The hulking security guard holds the door open for me; I'm almost too afraid to walk past him for fear his shadow alone will crush me, but I do, entering a room which is the polar opposite of the hallways outside. It's light and airy and inviting, all things which I as a designer can appreciate.

There's a tall male standing in a corner of the room, looking out the wall to wall windows, phone plastered to his ear. My heart catches in my throat and I have trouble breathing. Which is so not like me. I think it may be Jack Speed, but I could be mistaken. When the security guard tells me to take a seat, the man in the corner turns around, an irritated look on his face. It's Jack

Speed. Definitely Jack Speed. There is so much turbulence in his face when he looks at me, his eyebrows rising in surprise, as though I am more a mystery to him than he is to me.

"I'll call you back," he says into the phone, then lowers it from his ear and gives me an assessing look. He's got his suit jacket off, and he's wearing a powder blue shirt which clashes with his eyes, creating crazy little flutters within me. I could very well swim in the deep blue depths of his hypnotic eyes.

I've taken two steps into the room then stop when he turns and starts walking toward his desk, holding out a hand for me to sit. He has commanded me to take his direction without saying a single word. He takes a seat behind his desk and continues to watch me with an unusual level of interest.

"You're Ainsley's recommendation?" he asks, his voice dripping with disbelief. He says it like he's disgusted; I don't think he expected me to attend this meeting. He was possibly hoping Ainsley would send someone else.

"I am." I feel compelled to add that I am her best designer, but I don't. Arrogant does not look good on me.

"Ainsley also assured me that she would send her most professional designer."

I ignored his insult and held my tongue, pulling out my notebook from my messenger bag.

"I assumed I'd be meeting with Mr. Gable today," I told him, looking down at my notes. "Jack Gable."

"I prefer Speed."

He gives me a cocky smile and wraps his fingers on the desk like he's playing the piano. It's an odd interaction that's weaving all kinds of crazy on me.

"You're Jack Gable?" To my ears, this sounds more like a choke than a question.

"The one and only."

He realizes the minute he's struck me down with his identity, because my mouth refuses to move. I'm tongue tied. I'm mortified. And the level of embarrassment I feel is unparalleled. I'm sure that Ainsley is going to kill me anyway.

"What did you say your name is?" he asks.

"Olivia Kane," I whisper, after an endless pause trying to regain my voice.

"See?" He cocks his head and gives me a knowing look. "Kane & Gable. Somehow, I knew it wouldn't work. Call me Speed."

"Could this week get any worse?" I realize too late that my internal voice spoke aloud, and I find myself mentally kicking myself as he chuckles.

"Let's hope you're not as clumsy with your craft as you are on your feet."

So. Arrogant. I have a nerve to get up and walk out the door right then and there. Never mind that his face is doing things to my insides that should be considered criminal. And his body—let's just not go there. Instead, I fix him with a sweet smile and remind him that Ainsley is the best in the business, and she wouldn't stake her reputation on someone she didn't believe was capable of filling her shoes.

"Actually, you're right about that," he agrees. "She would never compromise on quality."

"Would you like to start with a tour of the place first?" I ask him.

He waves me off and tells me his personal assistant Selena will walk me around the club shortly.

"First, tell me a little about yourself," he says, and I'm taken aback. This isn't usual practice in my line of work. "About your artistic background," he is quick to add, leaving no room for misunderstanding. "I like to understand a person's professional background before I work with them."

I thought we'd already established that I was Ainsley's protege. Obviously, that's not enough to convince him.

"Graduate of Parsons. With honors. Interned at The Workshop, where I was mentored closely by Ainsley Winmore. My biggest project to date has been the Goldsborough. I also..."

He cuts me off abruptly.

"The Goldsborough. That was you?"

He leans forward in his chair, his interest

peaking. I can see he's impressed. The Goldsborough is only one of the biggest hotels in the state. The revamp and subsequent opening made waves in the design industry; it really was, in my estimation, the project that put me on the map in Ainsley's eyes. And the success of the project was also the thing that had given her the confidence to send me blind into other projects. And make me head designer. It was common knowledge at The Workshop that in the absence of Ainsley, I was second-in-command and heir apparent.

"It was," I concede.

"Well then, I can't wait to see what you do with this place."

◆ ◆ ◆

Jack rolls up his sleeves as he walks down the dark, narrow hallways, leading me out onto the mezzanine. He has decided he'll show me around rather than his assistant Selena, and I'm happy to get down to business so I can escape his presence as soon as possible. I walk behind him, trying to avert my eyes from the way his pants hug his hips and ass. The guy is full. And toned. Muscular. And arrogant. So damn arrogant.

He tells me his vision for the club, what he hopes to achieve, and the goals he has in mind. It's a multi-million-dollar renovation, but this doesn't seem to bother him as he continues through the club and points out features he'd like incorporated into the design process.

When we get to the open space located on the ground level, he leads me to a huge drafting table in the middle of the room and unfurls a set of plans, laying them out carefully on the table. He plucks a pencil out of a holder and starts laying the groundwork, explaining the aesthetics he's aiming for. I listen patiently, not interrupting him as he rattles off his wish-list. It's a ridiculous one at that.

"What do you think?" he asks, looking at me curiously.

"Can I be frank?" I ask him. I don't want to overstep here. Ainsley warned me Jack Gable was one of her dearest clients and she didn't wish to lose him. But I can't imagine that she'd agree to his ludicrous ideas. I have to keep him happy yet still do a stellar job of providing him with a world class club.

"Please do."

He crosses his arms against his chest and quietly waits. He is staunch in the way he stands, patient as I muster up the courage to go against the tide. There's something brewing in his eyes, but I can't discern quite what it is. I have to tread carefully here, but I can't compromise on my standards, either.

"You said you're aiming for high end, classy,

elite clientele. Animal cages and a pool are anything but. You'll attract the wrong clientele with that sort of set up."

He regards me for a long minute before he says anything. I think I've gone and put my foot in it again. This is going to be one of the hardest designs I work on if I have to be on constant guard with how forthcoming I am with the owner.

"You think so?" he asks.

"No, I know so." I say this with a false sense of bravado. He's an intimidating man, and the friendship he has with Ainsley adds to my anxiety.

"So you're confident enough to throw my ideas out the window and adopt your own?"

He's adopted a stern demeanor, his poker face not giving anything away. This could very well be my downfall. I'm already in the shit house, so I give him a short firm nod. He picks up the pencil and throws it in the tin, then folds up the plans and wraps an elastic band around them. Every movement he makes is designed to send a burst of nervous tension rushing through me. He aims to hit me where it hurts, and boy do I feel the punch.

"You've got the job," he says, handing me the plans. "Anyone who's brave enough to tell me where to shove my ideas deserves a medal."

And he walks away, leaving me gaping open mouthed at his retreating figure.

CHAPTER 8

JACK

Ainsley, a notable socialite who comes from old money and was left a king's ransom by three former husbands who predeceased her, lives in a sprawling mansion with lush gardens and a troop of servants. She greets me with a peck against both cheeks and wordlessly takes my hand, leading me out to the perfectly manicured gardens.

Over the years I've known her, she has become my go-to person when it comes to designing a space that people feel comfortable in and want to come back to again and again. I make it a point to visit her, even if only on a personal level, once or twice every time I'm on the East Coast, which isn't often enough. So, when she invites me for tea the afternoon after I've given The Workshop the green light to commence work, there's no way I'll turn her down.

She is the ultimate hostess, and she's set up a tea party fit for a King and Queen. I look at the spread curiously, wondering why she's gone to so much trouble—usually, we'll do lunch or dinner.

This is personal, I realize.

"Walk with me," she says, looping our arms together as she guides me through the garden. My breath catches in my chest at the sheer beauty she has created in her own back yard. It is a magical wonderland of perfectly trimmed hedges and great willows, with seasonal blooms scattered against the sandstone wall.

"You've created such a beautiful garden here, Ainsley."

She tilts her head slightly and regards me with a thoughtful look. There are unspoken words in her eyes, suffocating as they push their way to the surface. She invited me here because she wants to discuss something; she just doesn't know how to direct the conversation.

"What is it?" I ask, smiling at her.

"I hear there was some professional conflict between you and Olivia."

"There was," I tell her. "We've worked it out."

"You have? Olivia seems to think you two might encounter more problems down the track."

"She told you that?" I can feel the rise of my eyebrows when she says this. I'm surprised that Olivia would think there are still unresolved issues between us after our last meeting.

"She's worried the misunderstanding between you two—whatever it was—could affect our relationship. She was being honest with me, Jack, and I appreciate that. She doesn't want to be the one that drives a wedge between us because you and she can't get along."

I stop walking and sigh. I don't like complications. I don't like things which require too much effort where I don't have any to give. But I've given the idea of this collaboration the benefit of the doubt, and I'm willing to make it work, even if it means I stay out of Olivia's hair and let her take the reins. I'm actually looking forward to working with her, and what's more, I enjoyed our little spat, if you could call it that, because it's not often that I'm challenged. I'm so used to people knowing who I am and giving me what I want; with Olivia, that's all thrown out the window.

"She's not what I expected," I tell Ainsley. "And that could be because I'm so used to working with you. But I thought we'd put our differences behind us and moved past that."

"You two will get along just fine. You just need time to adapt to working with each other. Speaking of which," she says, looking at her watch, "Olivia should be here any minute now. I invited her to join us."

"You did what?"

"She's joining us for tea. You two will not leave here today without burying the hatchet and proving to me that this is going to work."

"Ainsley, there is no hatchet to bury. We've sorted out our differences," I tell her, just as the butler comes around the corner with Olivia on his heels.

She seems just as surprised to see me as I was to hear she'd be here today. She stops, probably thinks better of her reluctance to join us, and swallows her pride as she walks slowly toward us and kisses Ainsley's cheeks.

"I'm so glad you could make it, Olivia."

She pulls up a chair between Ainsley and me and plops herself into it without a word to me. Instead, she gives me a curt nod and a tight smile.

"Now, children," Ainsley admonishes. "We're all adults here. And you two are going to have to see eye to eye on something, because I'm invested in the both of you. Don't forget there's a deadline; every project must come to an end, then you can both go your own ways and hate each other as much as you want. So set aside your differences, whatever they may be," she raises her eyebrows in question, looking at us both, "and I don't know when you two found time to hate one other, since you've only just met. But I need you two to be on the same page for this project."

At that moment, the butler announces that Ainsley has a phone call, and she follows him into the house to take the call. I watch the beautiful woman walk away and wonder why she is so adamant on this project going ahead with the two of us—it would run so much smoother if we worked apart rather than together on this.

"Ainsley's got a lot of faith in your work," I say

once we're alone.

"I haven't let her down yet."

"Apparently not. She has only good things to say about you and your work. I may have been a little hasty in my initial judgement of you."

"Is that an apology?"

"No, definitely not. Just acknowledgement that I was wrong."

"There you go again…"

"You're too young to be head designer. So obviously, you're doing something right. I can't imagine that Ainsley would give you that role if you weren't deserving."

"Like I said, I've never let her down."

"You did when you kept cancelling my appointments," I remind her. "Where were you, anyway? I guess that's why I didn't take you seriously in that meeting. Young, female, kept blowing the meeting off…"

"That's a little sexist, don't you think? Taking my gender into consideration."

"Spin it any way you want, Olivia. A male never would have blown off a meeting that many times. It just goes to…"

"Jack," Ainsley interrupts, looking at me carefully. I can see she's gotten the tail end of the conversation and is putting things into context. She looks at Olivia anxiously, her eyes probing hers; and I finally understand the point of this tea. Olivia is as important to Ainsley as I am to her. She doesn't want to lose either of us. But nor does she want the permanence of any ill feelings between us.

"Olivia doesn't need to explain herself to anyone, but I need you tell me you can get past this and treat her respectfully based on the merits of her work. Tell me you can do this."

I look from Ainsley to Olivia. I'd already made up my mind that Olivia and I would be working together. I trusted Ainsley's opinion implicitly. I sat for a few moments, silently contemplating Ainsley's words, before I slid forward in my chair and moved toward Olivia. I held out my hand to her in a handshake.

"Hi. I'm Jack Speed, and I'm so glad to finally meet you."

CHAPTER 9

OLIVIA

"So what's the story with the suit?" Amy asks, as we tuck into boxes of Chinese takeout. She has her head buried in a box as she searches out the shallots, something she's done ever since we were kids. Amy has an unusual obsession with them.

"Which one?" I ask.

"There could only be one suit after meeting that man." She sets the container down and smacks her lips together. "You don't know a man in a suit until you've met Jack Speed."

"Please don't tell me you've developed a fascination with the man," I plead with her.

Amy has this habit of fixating on shiny new things. Until the next shiny new thing comes along. The only thing I'm sure she's never fixated on is my fiancé, Thomas. She, like everyone else in my family, never really warmed up to him in the way I had hoped everyone would. Which is oddly bizarre, because Amy and I have always been on the same page with every little detail of our respective lives. We like the same things, have the same hobbies, and we think alike. Thomas is the anomaly.

"You can't tell me you haven't noticed the man is a walking, talking piece of art, Olivia. I dare you to admit it."

"Regardless. Said piece of art is off limits. I cannot screw this up for Ainsley."

"Not talking about you," she mumbles, in between shoveling noodles into her mouth. "He's off limits to you because you're engaged. Or did you forget that extraordinarily life-altering piece of information?"

"No, I've not forgotten. Thanks for the unwanted reminder."

"Where is Thomas, anyway? For a man that's getting married, you sure seem to be seeing less and less of him these days."

"Work," I tell her. "He got a promotion that's keeping him busy most nights." I don't tell her that I'm glad for the distance his work has put between us. The constant reminder of how he roped me into an engagement I wasn't ready for has been grating on my nerves with every passing day, sending my anxiety levels skyrocketing.

"Have you guys thought about a date for the wedding?"

I put my container down and wash my food down with some water, then crack my neck and look down at our food. I've suddenly lost my appetite, even though I haven't eaten all day, and I'm not even a quarter way through.

"What's wrong?" she asks, setting her food down. Amy has an uncanny ability to tap into my moods and her own emotions usually mirror mine, especially when I'm not happy. She is loyal to a fault and fiercely protective of me.

"Can we not talk about this?" I ask her, getting up and pacing the room restlessly.

"Spill," she orders, and the look she gives me tells me there's no way she's going to get off my case until we do talk about it. I sigh and come back to the sofa, sitting across from her.

"I don't know that this is what I want," I tell her. "I know it's the natural next step in our relationship, but why am I not happy?"

Amy blinks rapidly. Like she's trying to hold back tears and a laugh at the same time.

"You don't have to marry him because he says you do, Olivia. It was wrong of him to spring this on you the way he did. He should have discussed it with you first."

"I think he knew I would have said no."

"That's not a valid reason for him to announce to the world that you're getting married. This is not an agreement. He's basically forcing your hand."

"I feel uneasy every time I think about it, Amy. I don't think I want this."

Amy sighs. "I can't tell you what to do; that's got to be your decision. But don't let him start making decisions and plans which require your input. Don't give him that power."

"It's just his timing really sucks. He couldn't have picked a worse time to announce this to the world. Like he knew there'd be no way for me to back out of the engagement because of my father."

"I dare say he planned it well, Ollie. He's been nagging you about the engagement for a while. Looks like he found an opportunity and he took it."

◆ ◆ ◆

When my phone rings as Amy and I are halfway through watching a silly rom-com we've probably seen about seven times before, I look down at the screen and freeze.

"Oh my God," I stutter.

"What?"

"It's him."

"Him who?

"Jack Speed. Why is Jack Speed calling me?" I ask, shooting her a confused look.

"On a Sunday night, no less." She sits up and anxiously fumbles with the remote as she tells me to answer it. But I can't. I can't answer. For some reason, I'm anxious and tongue tied and I don't want him to tell me that he won't be going ahead with the project. Even though we smoothed things over when we met at Ainsley's home, I don't really know how he really feels about working with me. This could be him pulling the plug.

The phone rings again, and I set it down on a side table, worried that I might be tempted to answer. I let the phone ring out and Amy and I are sitting looking at one another in confusion when a text comes through.

"Confirming your work on the club starts tomorrow?" I read out aloud, then flick my attention to Amy, whose jaw has just hit the floor.

"Doesn't he have a PA to deal with this sort of stuff?" she asks, frowning. 'Why is he calling you?"

I shrug and shake my head; I have no idea why he felt the need to call, but I can only imagine that after our last meeting, he just wants to make sure that we're good.

"Should I reply?" I ask her. She arches an eyebrow and gives me a smirk.

"Common sense dictates you should reply. It's not rocket science. Just tell him you'll see him tomorrow at whatever time you'll be there."

This is why I keep Amy around. What would I do without her otherwise? I shoot him a quick text to let him know I'll be at the club at 7am and put the phone down, half expecting it to chirp again. Amy is watching me carefully, dissecting every emotion, every blink of an eye, every single little thing that crosses my face to see where my head's at.

"You're not immune to him," she states, half statement, half scoff. She reads me so well, yet even I don't understand this power he has over me.

"Don't read too much into it, Amy," I tell her. "I'm just terrified I'll fuck this up."

"Exactly," she nods. "I haven't seen this much emotion from you in... ever."

CHAPTER 10

JACK

I knew even before she opened her mouth and rolled off her credentials and achievements that this was the designer I would be working with. By some stroke of fate, I happened to run into the girl from Central Park again, and this time she literally came with a bow. Hand delivered to me by one of my closest professional relationships—Ainsley Winmore.

Olivia comes in a few times a week to check up on the progress of the club. Most of the time, I'm not even here, attending to business elsewhere, but today I've made a point of being in the club when she comes by. I'm drawn to her in a way I don't even understand myself. We have a two-month deadline—ambitious, I know, but I insist on getting this club up and ready in time for me to meet my goals. I've given her free rein over the design concepts, and the two times we caught up to go over how things were progressing, I was more than impressed by what she'd managed to put together so far.

She points out planned features as we walk

through the club. The location of booths to optimize floor space capacity. The wood paneling and metalwork she hopes to incorporate into the bar, which wraps around in a full circle in the middle of the dance floor. She points out the LED lights built into the wall of the mezzanine and asks me if I'd be interested in a few other suggestions she has. Her ideas are solid and I'm not in the least bit concerned about the end product. I know she'll do a magnificent job.

"It looks like we're right on schedule," I comment, as we walk into my office. "You've done some impressive work."

Her smile singes my heart. Her goal was to make me happy and not let Ainsley down, and she's achieved both. She's well on her way to success with this project.

"If things keep up this way, we could even be done slightly earlier."

This is news to me. Unwelcome news. I don't want her work here to finish; I don't know why, but I've come to like having her here. "Like how much earlier?" I ask. I need to be prepared for this.

"A week, maybe ten days."

"That's great news," I lie.

She nods her head in agreement and tells me she has to get back to work. I watch her leave then swivel my chair until I'm looking out the window at the city below. I'm not doing myself any favors. The woman is engaged. By all accounts, happily.

She's going to be married soon. She'll finish this job and move on. I have my values; I may be an asshole, but I don't engage with women who are already in relationships. That isn't going to change now. But I can't bring myself to stop thinking about the beautiful klutz from the park who I had the misfortune of running into the day after she got engaged. I couldn't help but wonder —what if? What if I had met her a day before? A week? Even a month before?

She has not been in any social media posts since her engagement. From what I can see, Olivia is a very private person who doesn't like her personal life splashed all over the news and media. It looks like her fiancé, Thomas Thackeray is the exact opposite. He's the one who enjoys the limelight and will do anything to stay there. She on the other hand is low-key, a reluctant bit player in the drama that is unfolding around her.

"Boss, you have a 2pm," Selena reminds me, ducking her head into the room. I stand, button my jacket and head out of the office. Once I reach the mezzanine, the soft tinkle of female laughter reaches my ears. It's a sound I've become accustomed to. Even when she doesn't know I'm there, I stop and listen, breathing in her presence. She fits in to the landscape of my club like she belongs here.

I lean against the railing and look out at the main floor, watching Olivia as she speaks with a man in a hard hat. The head contractor. He says something and she laughs as she points out various stations around the room. Two men stand off to the side watching the interaction. I follow their eyes, which are cemented on Olivia, respectful and admiring. She is spinning a web all around her in which men and women alike are getting caught. Even Selena is crazy about her, and Selena doesn't like anyone.

It's at that moment that she glances in my direction, as though sensing me standing there watching her. Her hand goes to her neck in surprise, and we stand transfixed for a few moments, neither wanting to break the contact. It's only when the contractor speaks, repeating something he has said, that she shakes her head and looks away, as though shaking off my apparition from her mind. She concentrates her attention back to the work at hand, back to a world in which I have no place.

◆ ◆ ◆

I suffer in silence as the days wear on and Olivia becomes a slow combustible fire working her way into my life. I can't get her off my mind, and this has become a major problem for me. Sometimes it's easy to lose myself in her eyes when she looks at me during our interactions. I don't know if I'm reading too much in their bottomless pits, but I know there's something there. Something dangerous. Something which should be avoided at all costs. The woman is getting married, for fuck's sake.

In my crazy bid to inhale everything that's Olivia Kane, I've googled her. There's not much about her on the internet aside from the fiasco that was her fiancé dumping a premature engagement on her; I read this in an obscure thread on a reputable site that tells anyone who'll listen that the engagement wasn't a mutually planned one. It surprises me that Olivia would go along with something like that, as she doesn't appear to be a pushover.

Further research tells me what I already know; that Olivia is a very private person. Apart from what her fiancé has posted on the net, there's literally no trace of her in cyber space. Nothing that my PI can't fix.

Out of boredom, when my train of thought can't shut her out, I turn my attention to her fiancé Thomas Thackeray. He, on the other hand, has a strong social media presence. So strong in fact, that he seems to be lurking in every corner of high society. He seems to like his events. I can't help but notice that Olivia is missing off his arm at many of the functions he attends. And just like that, my attention is dialed back to the woman who's single-handedly turned my life on its head.

I need to shock her out of my system somehow

or forever pay the price for any mistake that I may make. I can't help the way I think about her. I'm sure it's just a major sexual attraction, easily dispelled if I just shut her out. I've been with a few women since I've met her, but every time we've crossed that road into a sexual encounter, I've found myself thinking more and more about Olivia. Imagining her, even. Imagining she's the one in my bed, between my legs, under my body. I imagine the filthiest things when I think about her, and I know it's only a matter of time before I do something I'll regret.

CHAPTER 11

OLIVIA

I'm measuring out the ideal space for the bar tops with the head contractor when Thomas waltzes into the construction zone with one of his colleagues, a man I've not met before. He glides into the room like he owns it and weaves an arm around my waist, nuzzling his face into my neck. He has caught me completely off guard, and I am gasping for breath as I look up, trying to collect my thoughts.

"My God," I breathe, "what are you doing here?"

"Can't a man come and visit his bride and whisk her away on her lunch break?"

"You should've called, Thomas. We really need to get through these measurements."

"I insist on taking you to lunch today, princess."

He does a bad pout and places a kiss on my forehead, hoping to get his way.

"If you're willing to wait, I'll be done in about forty minutes."

I flick my eyes toward the colleague, wondering if he'll be joining us for lunch. Thomas didn't even bother to introduce us, and I give him a tight smile before turning back to the benches to resume taking measurements.

A few minutes later, both distracted and irritated by his mere presence here, I turn toward Thomas when he calls my name and beckons me toward him for a photo op. My antenna goes up as I turn away and roll my eyes, then walk toward him.

"Thomas, I really need to get through what I'm doing," I say, advising him that the interruptions are not helping in any way.

"Just a few pics," he says, placing an arm around my neck as he pushes the phone into our faces for a selfie. He fires off three clicks, then moves us in the opposite direction for more photos.

"Thomas, you can't be taking pictures in here," I tell him, pushing the phone away. "This is a construction site; you shouldn't even be here."

"You run the site," he reminds me, as though that is all the validation I need to give him a free pass to do whatever he wants to do. As though it's an invitation to break every rule on safety in a work zone.

"Come on man, you heard your woman, let's wait outside for her until she's done."

Thomas stops mid-stride as he turns us in another semi-circle for a better shot, bristling at his colleague's words. I understand the exact implication of what the man has said and how Thomas has misconstrued the words as a slight against him. That another man would question his authority over his fiancé's causes his hackles to rise.

Thomas turns his eyes to the man and gives him a look that could spear him like a dagger. I cannot interpret what's going through his mind, but it can't be good, because he takes two steps toward the man, seething, then stops short and thinks better of continuing. Almost like a switch has flipped. He turns back to me and shoots me a dazzling smile, then turns to his friend again.

"It looks like my woman is too busy to have lunch with me today," he says, his tone deceptively friendly. "We'll let you get back to work, Olivia."

I watch the two men as they walk away, my mind a jumble with what just happened. Thomas has always, at the very least, been a pleasant man to be around. But today, I got a glimpse of his Dr Jekyll and Mr. Hyde. The change in him is so fleeting, but enough that I notice.

"You okay?" Tim asks. I turn towards Jack's head contractor and find he's come to stand next to me, his eyes full of concern. I'm not sure how much of the conversation he got, but it was probably enough by the look on his face. He shifts gears and I know he's only trying to make me feel better, but he fails miserably when he tells me he can finish the measurements on his own if I want to go to lunch.

I shake my head and sigh as I turn back to the bar. "I'd rather work on this and get it out of the way," I tell him.

"Olivia. You sure you're okay?"

Tim may have been hired by Jack Speed, and he may technically work for him, but he treats me like a baby sister, and I realize the protective nature of a brother is something I've missed out on in my life. I would've loved to have had an older brother.

"I'm fine," I tell him, unsure if I'm trying to convince him or myself.

"You're different round him," he tells me, a speculative look on his face.

"What do you mean?"

"I've never seen you as tense as you were when your fiancé was in here."

"This is my workplace," I remind him, but Tim merely shakes his head, telling me it's not that. Obviously, he sees something that I can't.

"You're different around him," he repeats. "And that's not necessarily a good thing."

CHAPTER 12

JACK

I find Olivia in the makeshift break room where my head contractor Tim indicated she would be. However, I don't expect that she'd be sitting alone at the table, her head resting on her arm like she is napping. I stop in the doorway and watch the steady rise of her back as she breathes in and out, and something deep inside me tugs at my heart strings. She is a delicate flower resting against the table, as the big bad wolf watches from the doorway.

Tim almost runs into me as he storms down the narrow hallway toward the break room, stopping short when he finds me standing in his way. He follows my eyes into the room, sees what I see, then fixes me with a worried look.

"I wasn't sure if I should wake her." I smirk, trying to make light of the situation. "I don't know how hard you've been working her."

It would seem my head contractor only has a sense of humor for Olivia, because he scowls and ignores me, looking again into the room. I notice how he's become more like a friend to her, weaving a protective shield around her. I know he's newly married and mad about his wife, so there's no danger in that department, but I can't get over how easy it was for him to infiltrate her trust when it's been an uphill battle for me. He stands looking at me now, a measure of suspicion in his eyes.

Olivia stirs, her hand reaching out for something on the table. She winds up scratching the surface before she retracts her hand again.

"I should wake her," he says. "The tiles are here and she was adamant she wanted to know the minute they arrived."

He turns into the room and I grab his arm before he can go any further. I must grab it too hard, because he gasps and looks down at his sleeve as it folds in my clutches.

"Let her sleep. I'll tell her when she wakes."

He gives me another irritated look before he shakes his head and turns to walk away. He'll protect Olivia at all costs, but he already knows there's no real danger with me. Not really.

"Tell me what?" Olivia says, lifting her head and wiping the sleep from her face. I enter the room and walk around the table to face her. Even in sleep, her hair looking like a bird's nest, she is still the most beautiful woman I have ever seen. So beautiful she takes my breath away and I have to remember to not stop breathing.

I turn to the coffee machine and make two

cups, setting one down in front of her before I take a seat.

"The tiles are here," I tell her, and her face lights up in excitement. I can see she's been waiting for this moment for a while. I settle a hand over her own before she rises, my eyes telling her to stay.

"They're still unpacking them, Olivia. There's no rush."

She's surprised me at every turn as this project has come together. Not least of which, the care she displays toward the maintenance and quality of all our products. She insists on overseeing loading and unloading all our construction materials. She won't accept even 1% variation or damage to any product. And she will not compromise on quality, even if she has to go to the trouble of sending things back multiple times.

"The boys will be waiting for me," she says.

She says the word boys to indicate her team. The boys... her boys... as in grown men, but they're her team. They may be on my payroll, but their loyalty is to Olivia. I've seen the way they treat and respect her. Some have put her on a pedestal. Others regard her with awe. I know that Selena for one is starstruck in her presence. Even though Olivia did not need to lift one finger to get anyone to like her. She just has a way about her, a presence that makes people gravitate towards her.

"Your boys can wait," I respond, fixing her with

a dark stare. I'm not immune to her charms, no matter how reserved they may be. "You look exhausted; you could do with a bit of a rest."

"Really?" She raises a hand to her hair and smooths it back, pinches her cheeks and looks down at her clothes, as though looking in a mirror to check what she looked like. Her actions are endearing and make me laugh, but I have to stop laughing when she looks at me with irritation.

"I'm surprised at how quickly you're getting through the project."

"Time is money," she reminds me. Like I could ever forget that. But time will only push us apart once this project is done. Maybe that's not such a bad thing, though.

Sitting here with her is making my heart beat erratically. All I want to do is reach out and run my hand through her hair, across her shoulder and down her arm until my hand is cemented to hers. I get the craziest urges when I'm around her, and that's saying something since I'm a man that's not easily affected by any woman.

"And my money is at your disposal, Olivia. You needn't rush the project."

She looks at me carefully as she sips her coffee. She's trying to read the underlying meaning behind my words, but my mask remains neutral as I return her gaze. This woman is doing unbelievable things to my heart.

"Still," she says finally, "I do have other projects to get back to."

"I appreciate that. You're doing remarkable work here."

"I'm glad you approve."

"I more than approve."

She shifts in her seat nervously and licks the side of her lip. Instinctively I understand that she's not nervous because of anything I am saying, but because of what my words are doing to her. She's just as affected by me as I am by her, and I lean forward in my chair, clasping my hands together in front of me.

"I should get back to work."

She is breathless as she speaks, but she doesn't make a move to leave. It's a dick move, and I swore I wouldn't do it, but I reach up and tuck a strand of her hair behind her ear. The silky soft strand is smooth against my skin, and I pause, not willing to move my hand away from her. She shifts uncomfortably away from my touch and rises quickly, sending her chair hurtling backward. She backs out of the room, her eyes never leaving mine, as though expecting me to do more. I rise and watch her go as she takes flight toward the work area. Even after I call her name, she doesn't turn. She doesn't afford me a backward glance as she leaves me and the danger I could do to the both of us.

CHAPTER 13

OLIVIA

Jack and I have called a silent truce. Silent because we never again speak of the conflict that besieged us when we first met. A truce because we are managing to get along just fine as our work together progresses. Of course, I don't see him all too often, but when he is around, we are able to put our differences aside and be civil to one another.

I'm surprised by how well our ideas on design are aligned. We share the same vision and goals for the club and vary rarely, if ever, disagree on a design concept. It helps that he's given me complete creative power over everything, and after our rocky start, I'm surprised that he actually has that much faith in me.

I've tried to avoid him as much as possible since the day my body sizzled at his touch. It hasn't been hard; I think he's trying to do the same as he stays away from the club. In a silly schoolgirl kind of way, I miss seeing him around, but deep in the depths of my soul, I understand that the distance between us is for the best.

When we stumble into a massive issue with the lighting and the problem stretches beyond fixtures, I decide I'll need Jack's opinion to see what he wants to do about the faulty electricals. I dial his number, but the phone just goes to voicemail. I head toward his office; it helps that Jack has given me free rein over the entire design process, including his office, which he has told me on numerous occasions I can use to hold meetings or make calls away from the deafening thump of drills and hammers and construction noise.

Sometimes I find myself gravitating toward the office just to have five minutes of quiet time where I can hear myself think. And I inevitably find myself drowning in Jack's scent, his heady, woodsy smell radiating throughout the office, a lingering reminder that he was once here. I recognize that it's become a smell I love and yearn for, perhaps even seeking it out.

The door is closed when I reach the office, and I am in such a hurry to get away from all the construction noise that I don't even bother to knock. I realize my mistake the second I fling the door open and take two steps into the room.

Jack is standing behind the desk, facing me, pumping and thrusting into a leggy blonde who is sprawled out across the desk facing him. He sees me immediately, and something dark crosses his face. It is raw and naked, a cloying desperation that filters from his eyes to my soul, bludgeoning me. I can feel the air seeping out of my lungs as I take in the scene and my jaw drops in surprise. I should walk out; I know I should. Just turn around and walk back out, but my feet are rooted to the spot as his eyes bore into me.

He doesn't stop. If anything, the moment it registers on his face that I'm standing there watching him, he thrusts at the blonde harder and deeper, a low growl escaping the depths of his lungs, his eyes never once leaving mine.

The woman doesn't see me. She is still clueless and quietly, surreptitiously, I grab the door and close it as I step back out of the room and take flight down the darkened mezzanine walkways. I stumble through the club, listen but don't hear what Tim is saying to me as I hurry past him.

Air. I need air. My lungs are suffocating, and I must look horrendous, because a concerned Tim is asking me if I'm feeling okay.

"Just… a headache," I mumble, grabbing my bag. "I'm heading home."

He shoots me a concerned look, and I'm grateful for the relationships I've nurtured while on this job.

"Give me a sec, I'll drive you home," he offers, but I shake my head and tell him I'm fine to drive. I shrug my way out of the club and walk, almost on autopilot, through the basement carpark until I get to my car, driving off quickly.

I'm horrified that I walked in on him in his own office and at what I saw. I feel ugly and dirty on the inside. I don't understand why I'm so upset about what's happened, but I can't get past the mortification running through my veins. It's my fault for barging into his office without knocking. Entirely my fault because I trespassed on his privacy. I never should have let his offer for me to use his office go to my head. Now I can never erase the awkwardness of what I've seen.

And then there's the delicate situation of how I'm really feeling deep inside myself. I'm hurt. I'm devastated. And with a sinking feeling igniting in my heart, I realize that I'm jealous. Tears threaten to invade my carefully constructed façade, and I swipe at my eyes as I drive the short distance home. When I pull up to the curb, I curse and let out an expletive; I've left my house keys in my briefcase at the club, which I overlooked in my rush to get out of there. Almost as if on cue, my phone vibrates and I jump.

It's Jack. I don't want to talk to him. I don't want to see him. I just want to sit with my broken emotions and analyze these foreign feelings surging through me. I don't want to deal with him, but I can't get into my house without my keys.

He is persistent. I answer on the fourth call, playing it cool.

"Olivia." His voice is curt. There is silence on

both sides as we both struggle for words. "You left your bag here. The contractor said you'd left."

"I've finished for the day," I tell him. I don't owe him any explanations.

"Do you want me to send your bag over to you?"

"If you could, please. I'm locked out of my house otherwise."

I can't believe how my traitorous heart softens at his voice. When I hang up, I get out of the car and sit on my front stoop, checking my emails as I wait for my keys to arrive. I refuse to let the situation affect me any further than it already has. I'm still sitting in this position fifteen minutes later when a sleek grey Maserati rolls to a stop next to my car. I am shocked into silence once again as Jack exits the car and walks towards me, carrying my bag. I'm shocked because he's here and shocked because—how on earth does he even know where I live?

Jack seems overly anxious. I can see it on his face. He can claim cool and calm all he wants, but when he's anxious, he frays at the seams.

"Sorry I kept you waiting."

"You didn't have to drive all the way out here," I tell him. I know he's a busy man. "I would've driven back."

"No problem." He shrugs and hands me my bag but makes no move to leave. I frown, questioning him silently.

"Thank you."

"Olivia..." he begins, but I cut him off immediately.

"There's an issue with the electrical work," I say, changing the subject. I don't want to discuss with him the events of the afternoon. "I'm sure you'll have to rewire now or risk significant damage down the road."

"Do what you need to do," he tells me.

"This might blow the budget."

"I've given you complete rein over the finances, Olivia."

This is true. The trust he has put in me is immense. But that's not enough to erase the hurt that dwells deep within me. I turn on my heels and start up the stairs.

"Olivia," he calls after me, and I know... I know that he wants to discuss what I saw this afternoon, but I won't allow it. I won't grant him the comfort of assuaging his guilt. It's none of my business what he does with his life, therefore I shouldn't allow his actions to affect me in any way.

"We'll meet with the contractor tomorrow at eight," I tell him, without turning back. I enter the building and close the door behind me without so much as a backward glance, knowing full well that he is still standing there watching me.

Once inside the house, I slump against the couch in resignation. My phone vibrates. I look at the screen and find it's Jack. I don't answer, but

I jump up and do a slow crawl to the window. He is still downstairs, pacing up and down a six foot patch in front of my apartment building. Something about that image tugs at my soul.

"Yes, Jack," I sigh into the phone.

"Don't shut me out," he says, his voice a firm plea.

When I'm silent for the longest time, he prompts me out of my haze by saying my name. I sigh, exasperated that I still have to deal with him when all I want to do is rest my head against a pillow and go to sleep.

"What do you want, Jack? Really?"

"Just to make sure you're okay."

"I'm fine. See you tomorrow at eight."

I have no intention of meeting him alone. I have no intention of spending any time with him other that what is absolutely necessary. And I absolutely will not allow him to infiltrate my heart again the way he did earlier today.

CHAPTER 14

JACK

I'm a handsome bastard. But I'm a bastard nonetheless. In my lifetime, I've been called every name under the sun. I can be a bastard and an asshole when the occasion calls for it. I don't think highly of women in general, and I have never committed to a relationship beyond two weeks. I don't lug around emotional baggage and I'm not interested in a happy ever after with anyone; I make my own self happy, thank you very much.

But the fact that I've let a woman get under my skin is telling in and of itself. Telling because I've never given a shit what anyone thinks of me. Until Olivia. The way she's avoided me at every turn for the past week speaks volumes about what she thinks of me. And now it's come to a point where Ainsley pays me an unexpected visit, her severe expression telling me something is definitely broken in the dynamic between Olivia and me. Ainsley has, in some ways, become judge, jury and executioner in our ongoing dramas.

"It looks like everything's coming together

beautifully," she says, clapping her hands together in delight as she walks through the club appreciating Olivia's hard work. We walk toward the office, where she takes a seat and settles in comfortably. She makes small talk before she drops her bombshell. For some reason, I'm nervous just having her in my office.

"I can see the major works have all been completed, and I hope they're to your satisfaction," she queries.

"Olivia did an excellent job of bringing everything together in substantially less time than I anticipated."

"I'm glad. And since the hard work has been done, someone else will now step in to put the final touches on this project."

She delivers her verdict as though handing me a slap across the face. Her words devastate me, and I struggle to mask my reaction so she doesn't know how affected I am by this news.

I straighten against the backrest and give Ainsley a curious look. It is unusual to switch designers so late in a project. Had things really become that intolerable for Olivia that she would forfeit her hard work and allow someone else to take the final credit for it?

"What's really going on here, Ainsley?" I ask her. She pauses and measures her words carefully, wondering how much to tell me.

"Olivia feels like she's done what she can here.

Everything else is just icing on the cake. She needs to start making preparations for her wedding."

Ainsley is studying me carefully, no doubt analyzing my reaction. There are words in her expression that she has not articulated. I wonder what's really going on here and what would cause Ainsley to jeopardize our relationship by pulling her best designer off my project.

"I need Olivia to see this job through to the end," I tell her.

"That's not possible," she tells me, and for the first time since I've known her, I feel my patience fraying before Ainsley. It's a first. And it's over a woman.

"You said you were giving me your best designer. I want your best designer to finish the job she was here to do. No one else." My voice is firm, and I speak with a sense of finality. I won't take no for an answer. Ainsley knows this side of me.

Her eyebrows shoot up, almost hitting her hairline, as she considers my ultimatum. She says nothing for the longest time, watching me with hawkish eyes as she dissects my words. She has to know that something has happened between us and that's why she's pulling Olivia off the project. She wouldn't jeopardize our relationship otherwise.

"I don't know what happened between you two," Ainsley says, standing up from her chair.

She decides to come clean, and I can't wait to hear what she says. "But for some reason, Olivia has asked me to pull her off this project. Now, I know that she would never ever let me down; what have you done to make things so intolerable for her?"

I feel my eyebrows fold in on themselves as I consider Ainsley's words. It pleases me immeasurably that Olivia was affected by that day when she walked into my office and saw me with another woman. A random woman. Whose name I can't even remember. A woman I wouldn't even recognize if I saw her walking down the street. Not like someone else I knew. Olivia's presence is embedded in my very psyche.

"I want Olivia to finish her work here," I reiterate. "I will stay out of her way until the work is finished. I give you my word."

◆ ◆ ◆

I make it a point to stay out of the club during the day and attend to other projects around the city. Olivia and I have very minimal contact, mainly via phone, and most of the time even that is through the head contractor, who relays messages between us as required. She doesn't know it, but I watch her on the surveillance cameras from my office at home. I watch her as she tucks a strand of hair behind her ear and discusses color schemes with other designers. I watch her move easily between the tradesmen, and the level of respect they have assigned her. I watch her interact with Selena, enjoying the easy camaraderie that has developed between the two women. And I follow her down the hallways as she passes through the mezzanine and crosses the threshold to my office. My eyes widen as she approaches my office door, and I watch in awe as she looks at the door, then places one palm to the wood, as though feeling me there, and lowers her head sadly. She lingers a few seconds too long, telling me she's just as affected by me as I am by her, before she lowers her hand and continues to walk down the hall.

◆ ◆ ◆

"What do you think?" Olivia asks, holding her arms out to encompass everything between us and turning in a circle. We are finally in a room together, a meeting which she has instigated. This is the handover. We are a day early on the projected timeline, and everything has come together beautifully. I know she was aiming to finish earlier, and I'm sure she would have—easily —but I know that our little misstep caused her some undue anxiety which in turn affected her work. Completely my fault, but we're still within the scheduled completion time.

"You've done a wonderful job," I tell her,

looking up at the vaulted ceilings with their crisscross design. It was a concept bound to spellbind. "Your vision is exceptional."

"I can't wait to see how it's received," she says, her enthusiasm infectious. "This club is going to be the hottest in town, I guarantee it." She is truly excited about the way that everything has come together to create such an amazing space.

"I need you at the opening, Olivia." I lower my eyes from the ceiling and give her my sincerest expression. I want to share with her the fruits of her labor. I want her to see first-hand the joy on people's faces when they walk into this space. I need her to see that. She shakes her head slightly, reminding me that she isn't a fan of social events.

"This isn't a social event, Olivia. This is the birth of your baby. I want you to be here to watch people as they flood through those doors and witness the appreciation in their eyes as they settle into their surroundings. You're as much a part of this as I am."

She gives me an uncertain look, then miraculously, her face breaks out into a dimpled smile. And this, this feeling right here, of seeing the happiness on her face, makes the wait for her to come around worth it.

CHAPTER 15
OLIVIA

I'm reluctant to accept Jack's offer of attending the opening of Oxygen8, but find myself pulled in by his insistence, Ainsley's pursed lips when I tell her I won't be attending, and Thomas's unreasonable fury at missing out on the event. Thomas is a media whore. That's the only way to describe him. For someone that works in finance, I don't understand how people actually trust him with their money; he's more an influencer than a Wall Street mogul. It doesn't make me love him any less, but I could do without the side of him that seeks out the limelight anywhere it's shining. Thomas literally had a conniption when I'd told him I wasn't planning on attending, especially because he realized he couldn't go either if the lead designer, who also happened to be his fiancé, wasn't going. It would just set tongues wagging unnecessarily.

Marcus, the security guard who has recently become my new best friend at the club, waves us in ahead of the milling crowd and wishes us a good night. Thomas pulls me into the club like a parent pulling along a wayward child, greeting people as we go. I'm constantly amazed by how many people he actually knows. Both men and women. The club manager shows us to the VIP table on the mezzanine, which looks out over the whole club.

"You've done a wonderful job," Thomas murmurs, his lips close to my ear so I can hear him over the thunderous sound of the music. He weaves a hand around my waist and pulls me closer to him then kisses the top of my head. He's already on his first drink, plucked off the tray of a passing waiter, as we stand at the railings and people watch. I sway gently to the music and his hand drops to my lower back, a bruising hold that means to remind everyone I'm his.

When Ainsley arrives with my father, they sit at our table and I leave my place at the railing to join them. I know they're here for the sake of appearances and will only stay a short while before they leave again. In separate cars. God knows I've tried over the years to get these two together, but it's never happened for them. Instead, my father and the woman who helped shape me into the person I am today have remained close friends throughout my life.

"Where's Jack?" Ainsley asks. "I didn't see him on my way in."

I shrug, my face a placid mask when his name is mentioned. I don't want to tell her that I scoured the crowds with my eyes for almost an hour and didn't see him. I don't want her to read the disappointment in my eyes; if I had to be honest with myself, I was looking forward to seeing him tonight, in what would probably be the last interaction I would ever have with him. I wanted that one last look at him. That one last conversation where I could drown in the rich syrup that is his deep, commanding voice, before I left this club and never came back. After tonight, Jack would no longer be a part of my life. My work here was done. And I could turn a new page and concentrate on my own life moving forward. Ainsley has already slated the smaller jobs for me so I can start preparing for my wedding. Which, truth be told, I'm happy to delay as long as I possibly can, but Thomas seems to be working on a timeline and is pushing for a Spring wedding.

"Everything you've done with the place is remarkable," my father says, clasping my hands in his. "You've done a hell of a job with it, and I'm so proud of you."

"This deserves a toast," Ainsley pipes up. I catch Thomas's attention and motion him over as we clink our glasses together. "To Oxygen8's success, and the amazing work Olivia has done here."

"And to even greater collaborations," my father adds.

◆ ◆ ◆

It's not lost on me that I don't get overly jealous when Thomas dances with other women. I'm not the jealous type and I've never had cause for concern when it comes to him. When Ainsley and my father take their leave, I beg off dancing and Thomas takes his place on the dance floor as I chat to a few passersby at the table, then continue to watch the happy revellers from the mezzanine. Thomas jumps from patron to patron, weaving his magic with everyone he comes in contact with. He doesn't fail to engage any and all as he moves through the crowds, mesmerizing both men and women alike. Tonight, he's wearing black dress pants and an electric blue shirt that sets off his eyes. His hair is almost the same color as mine, with the light brown strands slicked back from his forehead. I'm told he had a head of blonde curls as a child, which explains his fair coloring now. Even in his late 20's, he's still managed to retain a boy-like charm to match his cherubic features. He has a light sprinkling of golden-brown hair matted against his cheeks, and he's handsome in that way that old movie star types are, the sort of handsome which only makes him accessible to a certain degree. He reminds me of a young Paul Newman, right down to the hooded eyes and charisma.

Jack still hasn't made an appearance, an unusual concept on opening day of an establishment, but not altogether unheard of.

The night is still young, and the club is full to overflowing with excited patrons as the evening progresses. The clientele this venue has attracted is the exact sort of high-class patronage Jack anticipated, and I can see the four bartenders cannot keep up with demand.

"You owe me a dance."

Thomas comes up behind me and wraps his arms around my waist, nuzzling into my neck.

"You know I'm a hopeless dancer."

"You're an amazing dancer. Just one—for my sake. So I can show you off."

His lips trail up the side of my neck until they land on my lips, coaxing me into getting what he wants.

"Just one dance," I warn him. I won't be roped into becoming a ringside attraction for anyone.

"Just one," he mumbles, in between kisses against my skin, before he leads me toward the dance floor.

CHAPTER 16

JACK

My eyes are glued to the screen. I've been watching her all night, and I haven't been able to move my feet in the right direction and into the club. Everything else seems to be running smoothly, and I'm thankful for the amazing staff I've hired as my eyes swivel between the multiple screens then settle on the one with her image on it.

Her fiancé is leading her to the dance floor, his hand at the small of her back. She's wearing a short gold dress that blends so seamlessly with the design of the club that she could easily pass as a permanent fixture. They don't have to push through the crowd. Thomas is a people person, a trailblazer for whom the crowds part as he heads toward the arena. I notice the fact that he is in the company of Olivia only lends to his credibility, and I wonder how much of their 'premature engagement' was him ladder climbing. Olivia is the kind of woman every man wants on his arm and every woman wishes to emulate.

Her hair is pulled back in a high ponytail, a few

loose strands curling down the side of her face. Her strappy heels are so high, I have concerns for her back, but she rocks them as though she's wearing flats. Her makeup is flawless, a radiant blush coating her face as she takes her place on the dance floor. I can see that she's uncomfortable. They're in the middle of the floor, and people start moving away, gathering around them in anticipation. No one stops dancing at a nightclub, but this is obviously a show no one wants to miss. Knowing the way Olivia feels about publicity and her own privacy, I'm never more grateful that I've insisted on a phone free policy in the club. I know the sort of clientele whose patronage I want would appreciate the fact that they are in an environment where they can relax and be themselves without having to worry about the click of a camera.

I sit behind my desk and watch as half the club comes to a standstill. Everyone's watching Olivia and her so-called fiancé gyrate and strut their stuff across the dance floor. I have to admit, they make a mesmerizing couple. They're easily comfortable with one another, as though they've done this countless times before, shutting out the rest of the world as they become consumed with each other. Olivia smiles at Thomas, but her smile doesn't reach her eyes. It's a different sort of smile, and if I didn't actually know what her delighted smile looks like, I would've missed it.

The spectators are in awe of the couple, and I can now so clearly see what the other side sees; how easy it would be for one to assume this couple is the match of the century, so engrossed are they in each other. One couple, two beautiful people, their souls entwined. Thomas Thackeray is tall, slender without being wiry, and astonishingly good looking with his scruffy light brown hair and blue eyes. I can understand how any woman would be smitten with him based on looks alone, but I can't say that Olivia seems taken with him. I imagine his looks are what have played a pivotal role in advancing his life's ambitions.

I'm watching carefully, unaware I've been holding a breath, all pent-up tension and anxiety, when Thomas turns Olivia on the dance floor and comes in from behind her, one hand encircling her waist as he glues his chest to her back and his other hand slides down her thigh. He does it in a way that's sexy without being lewd, and the whole club erupts in shouts and yells, urging them on. When Thomas moves his hand toward the hem of her dress and starts to slowly lift it, Olivia smiles wider and pushes away from him, doing a solo strut. And I take that move to be exactly what it is; her disapproval of Thomas trying to lift her skirt for the sake of gaining everyone's attention at her expense.

My mouth twitches, and I feel a deep stab in

the pit of my stomach. A feeling of raw anger overcomes me as I realize how jealous I am of his hands on her. It's a foreign feeling to me, this jealousy, not one I've ever felt toward anyone in all my thirty-two years. And I can't say that I like it.

◆ ◆ ◆

"That was quite a show you put on there," I murmur into Olivia's ear, as I move to greet her with a kiss on her cheek. I take advantage of the fact that the whole club is watching us and use this opportunity which could be my one and only chance to ever inhale her scent at such close proximity. "Thank you, we'll probably be booked solid for the next few months thanks to your display."

She pulls back, holds me at arm's length, and hides her scowl behind a smile. She's fuming but hiding it well, and I know it's because I've hit a nerve. Thomas is using her to climb even higher on the social ladder. In some shape or form, subconsciously, she probably already realizes this but hasn't been able to find a way to extract herself from him. She loves him, I have no doubt, but is she in love with him? I doubt it.

"This is my fiancé Thomas," she introduces, pulling him toward her. Thomas's eyes start fawning all over me even before he thrusts his hand into mine. I grip his in a vise-like grip to show him how real men do handshakes, smile because I know all eyes are on us, then drop my hand and listen to what Thomas is not saying. All I can see in his eyes are stars and opportunities. He knows exactly who I am. He knows I've made the '40-under-40' Rich List and he probably already knows my net worth. Thomas Thackeray is the kind of man who does his research and does it well. Think... gold digger.

Before he can make his move and pitch his case to me, I move my eyes back toward Olivia and thank her for coming, then move to the bar and order a drink. I take a sip and push the glass back toward the bartender before moving back to the couple. Thomas has his attention on someone who's just walked into the club and steers himself that way, leaving Olivia chatting with a woman she seems to know well. I catch her eye and nod in the direction of the bar, where I take a stool and wait for her.

"I can see you're in a mood tonight," she says, hopping onto the stool beside me. Her dress rides up, giving me a glimpse of skin. I suck in a sharp breath and my hand automatically shoots out to her knee. I rest it there for a moment, and her eyes become fixated on that hand that is now scorching her skin. I pull down the hem of her dress and withdraw my hand. Her eyes catch mine, and she is speechless but she recovers quickly. As though nothing happened. She's acting as though she's not as affected by that touch as I am. She crosses her legs and motions for a bartender to give her a drink. It's champagne all round tonight to celebrate, but she decides to ask for a dirty martini. My mouth is salivating thinking of all the dirty things I want to do to her, and none of those things have anything to do with a martini. None of those filthy things should even be thought about in a crowded club like the one we're in now.

Avoiding her gaze, I look down at my drink, turn the glass around on the counter contemplatively, then lift it to my lips. My eyes are back on her and her alone as I down my drink in one swallow. She rakes her assessing gaze over me, searching for something I can't quite make out. We may have moved on from our awkwardness over her walking in on me mid-sex with a woman whose name I don't even remember, but she's still cautious around me. Maybe even a little relieved that we'll probably never see each other again after tonight.

"So what's next for you?" I ask.

She's silent for the longest time, perhaps wondering how to tread here. She doesn't owe me any answers; she's fulfilled her part of the bargain and produced an amazing masterpiece in this club, so she knows any curiosity I aim her way now is all me.

"I have a few small projects lined up."

"Downgrading?" I ask. "Or in need of a break?"

"No," she replies, lifting her chin defiantly. "I'm planning my wedding actually."

She hops off her stool, telling me in no uncertain terms that the conversation is over. I grab her as she bids me goodbye and turns to leave, and her eyes lower to my hand as it digs into her arm. I know she feels the spark of electricity that sizzles between us in that one touch.

"Don't marry him if you don't love him," I warn her.

She gives me a cold look, shakes her head in disbelief, then turns and walks out of my life.

CHAPTER 17

OLIVIA

I'm well into the planning stages of our wedding and Thomas is throwing up roadblocks at every turn. I want a small, intimate wedding, and he is pulling out all the stops and today he's insisting on 800 guests. And that list is only expanding. The thought of having that many people at my wedding terrifies me, and I'm suddenly wondering if eloping is an option. Thomas almost chokes on his water when I suggest this, then turns to look at me like I've grown two heads.

I'm getting ready for tonight's charity ball, one of only a handful I will attend throughout the year in support of breast cancer awareness. The disease took my mother's life prematurely, and I feel strongly that more can be done to combat this silent killer and support women who are suffering from it. Thomas sits on the bench seat at the foot of my bed and I watch him in the mirror as I attach my earrings. He looks exquisitely handsome in his dark tuxedo and red bowtie, and I can't help but admire the way his eyes crinkle when he smiles back at me. He's come to pick me up from my place, arriving well in advance so we can discuss the latest plans for our wedding. None of which he's on board with.

"I've already told you I don't want a big wedding, Thomas. You're the one that's rushing into this, I think the least you can do is let me dictate how many guests."

He shakes his head emphatically, refusing to give in to my requests. He won't have a bar of it, and he insists on a big wedding and a lineup of celebrities who he believes will legitimize our relationship. His words, not mine.

"I don't even know what that means," I tell him, turning around to face him, a deep fury threatening to erupt from within me. "Why would we need to legitimize our relationship? And there is no way… no way," I emphasize, "that I'm allowing paparazzi into my wedding. That's non-negotiable."

"You know that all eyes will be on us, Olivia. We can't not give the press anything," he admonishes.

"Yes, we very well can. I don't want my picture plastered all over the newspapers."

"And you know how important networking is to my career. My business and my future relies heavily on what I give the public."

"Your future," I scoff, grabbing my clutch off my dresser. It's always all about Thomas. His life. His career. His future. His way. We're both successful professionals, and we both come from monied backgrounds, so I don't understand why this ladder climbing is so important to him. And what's worse is that it's at my expense. The one thing I won't compromise on is my privacy. My life is my own, and that's the way I want it to stay. I don't want to share every facet of my life with the rest of the world. I refuse to do so. This is why I keep only a very small circle of friends—so my life remains my own without every detail being spilled out in the gossip columns or on the front-page news.

"We're going to be late," I tell him, walking out of the room.

"This conversation isn't over," he says, following close behind me.

"It is for now. We can talk more later; right now, I want to attend this event, and I want to do it with a smile on my face."

◆ ◆ ◆

I walk into the grand ballroom with a smile on my face and frost in my heart. I am seething that Thomas argues with me all the way to the venue, even after I politely request that he shut up. He went on and on and on about keeping up appearances, and what would people think, and why was I being so difficult? By the time we got to the venue, I was just about ready to get back into the limousine and direct the driver to take me back home. The only thing that stopped me was that I'd been to this event every year running since I was seventeen. For seven years, I'd been a fixture at the charity auction, flitting between attendees who were willing to open their purses and pledge big for this cause that was so close to my heart. For the last few years, I'd served on the board, one of my few concessions in dealing closely with the public and the media because it was for such a great cause. I took my contribution seriously, and I wasn't about to let Thomas sour my mood tonight.

Thomas is off mingling with the guests even before we've stepped into the ballroom, networking and showing off his skill as a social butterfly. Internally, I'm a little sad and confused at the way he's behaving, but silently glad for the reprieve I get from his arguing over wedding guests. I've had to sit through that for the past half hour, and it's left me feeling exhausted.

"Olivia..."

A deep husky male voice addresses me by name from somewhere behind me. Even without turning around, I already know who it is from the sound of his voice. How can I not? My lips part in surprise, and I feel my body stiffen. When I turn around, I add breathless to my state as I take in Jack's piercing blue eyes and wavy brown hair. If it's at all possible, he's bigger than before, filling out his suit, looming larger than life itself. He is a hulking whale and I am a tadpole next to him. He's more handsome, more dashing, more everything than I remember him being. And his presence slices at my heart, causing it to beat rapidly.

His hair is slightly longer at the back, a thick scruff curling over his neck, and I realize the time that has passed since I last saw him. It's been maybe four months or so. I won't lie and say I don't think about him from time to time, but it's always been in the sort of way that one thinks of an old friend.

"I wasn't expecting to see you here." I stutter. I actually stutter. And buckle. Almost falling over myself as words evade me. He gives me a mesmerizing look, his eyes dancing with... happiness? He looks happy to see me, and I can't say my heart isn't doing a happy dance or two around the room.

I'm standing tongue-tied in front of him when I'm suddenly taken by surprise when arms wrap around my waist. I'm pulled back into a male body, and recognize Thomas by his scent. He cradles one side of my neck with one hand and pushes a kiss to the other side as he looks over my shoulder.

Thomas tightens his grip around my waist and extends a hand in Jack's direction. There is a quiet storm brewing in Jack's eyes. "It's good to see you again, Jack," Thomas says, steering me away from Jack. "Now if you don't mind, there's someone I'd like my fiancé to meet."

Thomas's hands around my waist are a punishing shackle. He's going to leave bruises if he holds on to me any harder, and I give him a confused look as he steers me to a quiet corner of the room out of earshot of everyone else.

"You two seemed friendly enough," he says.

I'm even more confused than I was a moment ago as I consider his words. The look on his face is thunderous, something I've never seen in him before. Thomas is jealous. And this is a new side to him that I don't think I like.

CHAPTER 18
JACK

When Thomas whisks Olivia away, I think he finally understands the danger I pose to him. No one can misconstrue the look on his face when he marshals her away from me. The dynamic of their relationship does not include jealousy. Olivia is comfortable enough in her own skin not to worry about Thomas with other women. Thomas has never seemed like the jealous type, but it could be he feels like he's losing control of the hold he has over her. I know his type. Losing Olivia would be a massive loss for a social climber such as himself. He's going to avoid it at all costs.

I'm not out to break them up or come between them. I'm just trying to understand this pull I have toward her. Toward protecting her. And I can't understand why I haven't stopped thinking about her since that last time I saw her in the club.

I follow Olivia with my eyes, watch as he backs her into a corner and has a short, stilted conversation with her. She is too respectful to make a scene or allow anyone to see her discomfort, so she plasters a smile onto her face and carries on as though nothing has happened, even when I see the empty despair in her eyes. I don't know why she doesn't simply walk away from him.

"Jack, darling."

I whirl around and find my date, Morgan Creed, at my side. She places her hand on my arm and guides me towards our place at a nearby table, reminding me that dinner is being served. Morgan is the reason I'm at this charity event. Actually, no. Olivia is the reason I'm at this event—Morgan is the vehicle that got me here. I only agreed to come as her date because I knew that Olivia would be here and I wanted to see her. I've done a good job of staying away from her. I could have gone through with any one of the hundred scenarios I had thought of to run into her, but in the end, I'd kept away to avoid appearing like a stalker. But when this night quite literally fell in my lap, I'd known I had to come, if only to satisfy my own urge to see Olivia.

By sheer dumb luck, my seat gives me a great view of Olivia's table a few feet away from ours, even if it is only a back view. But it gives me great insight into the nature of her relationship with Thomas. After dinner, and as the speeches are being delivered, I glue my attention to the rise and fall of Olivia's breath where she sits in front of the stage. I watch as Thomas leans over, brushing a hand across her back, and whispers something in her ear. I notice how her body stiffens and how she lifts a hand to play with her earring nervously. I watch as Thomas's gaze roams around the room, settling on some attendees longer than others. And there is no way I can miss the curt way in which Thomas addresses the man sitting to Olivia's right when he seems to be paying her too much attention. Something isn't right here, and I cannot understand why Olivia continues to play along with this charade.

Things go from bad to worse when the entertainment portion of the night begins. I glide around the ballroom floor with Morgan leading the dance and watch as Olivia stands chatting to a few people at the edge of the floor. Thomas is nowhere to be seen, and I see Olivia's discomfort as she tries to hold herself together. Analyzing the couple so closely, I realize I'm seeing something the world is not really seeing. For all his fluff and obsession with the media, Thomas has done a good job of creating and perpetuating the image of marital bliss the public is so hungry for. He's understood what the masses need and he's given it to them on a silver platter, albeit at the expense of Olivia's privacy and happiness.

When Thomas returns from wherever the hell he was, Olivia is being spirited across the dance floor by a man who I know is one of her father's oldest friends. I watch on in curiosity as Thomas wordlessly breaks into their dance, leaving the man with a befuddled look on his face, and slides her into a dizzying spin across the floor. I can see from the look on her face, which again she tries to mask, that she is horrified by what's happening. It's hard for her to hide the subtle way that Thomas's hands dig into her arms, or the menacing way he leans into her ear and whispers something. She starts to say something, but Thomas smiles as though conducting a normal conversation and cuts her off. He's always smiling for the benefit of others, hiding beneath a thin layer of evil that his boyish charm has hidden well from the world for so long.

I want to go over there and steal her away from him. I want to protect her from his special kind of madness, but I don't know how to do it without igniting her ire. She's already made it clear that she wants nothing to do with me. She won't even accept the friendship I've offered her, and so I continue to watch and wait from a distance, biding my time.

"Jack, fancy seeing you here."

I turn and come face to face with Ainsley Winmore who, although addressing me, has her laser sharp focus on Olivia. She looks from me to Olivia, then back at me again, a question in her eyes. Ainsley is one of the smartest women I've ever met. I find it hard to believe she wouldn't have noticed how Thomas mistreats Olivia.

I take the older woman's hand in my own and

place a kiss against her knuckles. She is not only a business associate, but she is also a good friend. What's worked for us is that we can so easily compartmentalize so that the business side of things stays in that realm, and our personal lives are for our enjoyment and a chance to catch up without the stressors of our work.

"Ainsley."

"I don't think I've ever seen you at a charity function," she remarks, coming to stand beside me after I've introduced her to Morgan.

"You know I prefer to do my bit rather quietly."

She nods in understanding then turns her attention across the room again. "What do you suppose that's about?" she asks, lifting her chin in Olivia's direction. She knows the girl well enough to read the tension radiating off her body.

"I couldn't say," I murmur, looking at Ainsley. She gives me a knowing look that tells me she doesn't for one moment believe me.

"We should meet sometime next week," she says. "For coffee. At my house in the Hamptons—I recall you said you were looking for a property there."

"I am."

"You should come and have a look at my home before it goes to market. Absolute beachfront. Private. Just what you're looking for."

Ainsley is up to something. She rarely—if ever—sells any property. But who am I to argue if she has what I could possibly want?

"Have your PA talk to mine; I have an opening next Friday afternoon."

CHAPTER 19

OLIVIA

Thomas's moods are giving me whiplash. No sooner has he whisked me away from the man who has been my father's best friend for decades than he has me backed into a corner of the room and is berating me like I'm a child. I am mortified. I maintain a smile on my face, even as his fingers dig into my arms menacingly. He's no better; he puts on a good show for people as he continues to nod and smile as he greets people whilst simultaneously 'putting me in my place.' In all the years I've known him, Thomas has never so much as shown me this side of him, and I struggle to identify what it is that has triggered this change in him.

"You stay right by my side," he whispers close to my ear. "I don't want you near any man here tonight."

I'm taken aback, my eyebrows shooting for the sky as I try to keep the shock off my face. The way he's talking to me is as though I've done nothing but entertain men all night, and I'm stunned hearing the words out of his mouth.

"Thomas..." I try to defend myself but he doesn't let me finish. He gives me a warning look and guides me across the room towards the auction, where he literally delivers me to the chair next to my father as though for safekeeping and tells me he'll be back.

My father takes one look at me and stiffens. It's no secret he doesn't much care for Thomas, and the way he looks at me now when I tell him everything's okay guarantees that his mistrust of Thomas has not been misplaced. I will do anything to protect my father, but I've always found it hard to contain my emotions around the man who reads me like a book. For so many years, it's been just him and me, with Ainsley playing a pivotal role in my life also. The three of us have come to know each other so well, it becomes hard at times to know where one personality begins and the next ends. We are so synchronized, it's hard not to understand what's going through each other's minds.

"You'd tell me if something was wrong, wouldn't you?"

I nod, and my father is not convinced, but he flattens his lips into a tight line and says nothing, opting instead to remain silent.

"Will you be bidding on anything tonight?" he asks, changing the subject.

"I can't believe the caliber of items that have come through here tonight," I tell my father, turning excitedly towards him. "I think this is going to be our biggest collection yet."

My father laughs, his eyes crinkling at the edges as he dives into my enthusiasm.

"What will you be bidding on?"

"I'm eyeing a Keating. Chrissy Maran has donated a few lovely pieces."

"What about that new artist. Gabe McFadden... isn't he the artist you discovered in Central Park?"

I nod my confirmation. "His work is amazing. I can't believe he'd never considered monetizing his work."

"There was a piece about him in today's paper. Small, but it's something. The author made a comparison to Pollock."

"I wouldn't be surprised, he's very talented."

"Who's very talented?" Thomas asks, coming back to sit with us.

"One of the artists who's represented here tonight," my father tells him, watching Thomas carefully.

"Not that Gabe McFadden, I hope," Thomas remarks.

"Precisely the man."

We watch Thomas's face contort into an expression of distaste.

"His work lacks dimension," Thomas says, and even though he's entitled to his opinion, I can't help but giggle.

"That's not what this morning's paper said," I

point out. In the presence of my father, I never fail to feel brave. I feel like I can fly, then fall, and he will pick me up each and every time. I feel safe and loved and warm. I feel complete. All the things I know I don't feel with Thomas. Which could explain why we haven't moved in together yet. Which could explain my reluctance to rush into a wedding. And which could so obviously be all the signs I need to see to make the right decision for myself.

Thomas scowls and tells us both the artist is a one hit wonder and will amount to nothing. I'm not entirely sure why he feels so threatened by all the men in the room tonight, but something is definitely going on with him.

"The auction's about to start," my father says, and we settle back into our seats as the auctioneer takes the podium and starts knocking off item after item.

When my father purchases a Gabe McFadden original, he sits beaming that he's won the bid, while on my right, Thomas sits cursing and mumbling under his breath, loud enough for me to hear. And he just won't stop.

"What on earth is your problem tonight, Thomas?" There is quiet fury surfacing within me.

"$20k for that lousy piece of garbage?"

"Would you kindly keep your voice down! You're making a scene."

"I think it's time for us to leave."

Thomas rises out of his seat and holds his hand out to me. He's basically interrupted the whole auction and dug his own grave; the whole room has turned our way in interest. I'm beyond horrified at the attention that he's thrown on us, and even more so because I'm so closely linked to the foundation. This is not the sort of publicity anyone needs, let alone a charitable organization.

"The auction's not over yet, Thomas." My father's voice is terse, brooking no argument.

"We're leaving."

"My daughter advises me on all my art acquisitions; you know that. If you need to leave, do so. I'll make sure that Olivia gets home safely."

Thomas is not happy at being dismissed, but even he now understands the folly of his ways. He exits the room quietly, and the auctioneer waits a moment for the commotion and whispers to subside before he resumes the bidding. With everyone's sole focus on me, I feel like I want to just slide into my chair and disappear.

"Let's try to enjoy the rest of the night, shall we?" My father bumps my shoulder and gives me a warm smile. "There'll be plenty of time to talk about this tomorrow."

CHAPTER 20
OLIVIA

I look in the mirror above the vanity. I don't know what I see. It's almost as though a stranger is looking back at me. Overnight, something has changed in me. Something has shifted, and I'm not sure what that is. All I know is that I'm miserable, and I'm still nursing a broken heart over the embarrassment that Thomas caused us last night.

I don my trainers, tie my hair up in a ponytail and sit on the bed. I hit replay on my voicemail. Thomas has called fourteen times since last night. Each time the answering service kicked in, he'd hang up. Fourteen times he called. I wasn't sure how we'd reached the place we now stood at; we'd had a steady, stable relationship for two years. But lately, Thomas has changed. There is something different about him—an untamable madness that not even I can contain. I've never seen him act the way he did last night—spoilt, brattish, sulky. This was not the Thomas I had known and cherished for years. I had spoken to, joked and debated with men on numerous occasions and never been subjected to such outbursts. So, I couldn't understand why all of a sudden, he had developed a complex over me simply talking to other men.

I lock my door and tuck the keys into my pocket as I make my way down the stairs. Every step I take is deliberate, almost mechanical, as I stroll across the road to Central Park. I start a slow jog, then pick up my pace, passing hundreds of joggers and early morning walkers leisurely enjoying their Saturday morning. I run for thirty minutes before I end up at the pond. I stand there quietly, looking out over the calm waters, breathing deeply as I try to catch my breath. I double over, my hands on my knees, as I fight off a stitch and do some easy breathing exercises.

"Good morning, Olivia."

I turn slowly and face Jack, losing my breath all over again. His blue eyes are like crystals within which my reflection resides. His five-day growth is just that little bit longer, and I think I like it this way. He is devastatingly handsome, sucking the soul right out of me as I stare at him.

In another life, in another time and place, Jack would have been everything I wanted in life and more. I wondered at the hand of fate that could bring him into my life the day after I got engaged. Life had a mysterious way of dealing out winning cards. And none of those cards seemed to make their way into my hands. "So that's the fiancé," he says. He's met Thomas before, so when he says this now, I understand the true meaning of his words for what they really are. He's asking me why the hell I'm still with a man who doesn't seem to measure up to my standards.

"What are you doing here?"

"The same thing you are. We've really got to stop meeting like this."

I look him up and down, notice the lack of jogging gear, and point this out to him.

"I'm not here to jog, Olivia. I'm here to see you."

The muscles in my temples contract as I watch him, speechless, realizing we're touching on dangerous territory. There would be no coming back from whatever happens here today.

"How did you know I'd be here."

"Does that matter?" he asks, and for the first time, I detect a note of vulnerability in his voice. There is a reason why he's here. He walks toward me, then right past me and down to the willow shading the pool of water before us. "Let's sit for a bit," he suggests, and involuntarily, my legs move to join him on the grassy hill under the willow.

"You knew, right back when we first met, that I was committed," I tell him.

He nods. "I did."

"So why do you keep invading my life this way? You're only complicating things."

"There'd be nothing to complicate if you and Thomas were solid, Olivia. But I'm having a hard time understanding what it is exactly that you're committed to."

"That doesn't concern you."

"After last night, I'm making it my concern. I saw the way he treated you."

"Again, that's none of your business."

Jack looks out over the pond into the distance, his blue eyes fixed on a point beyond the ducks diving into the water. I've never seen him out of a suit, but today he wears loose jeans and a black t-shirt which shows off his well-defined muscles. He looks all sorts of yummy to my eyes.

"Truth be told Olivia, I don't know why I'm here. I've thought about you every single day since that last meeting at the opening of the club. I've etched every single moment of our time working together into my brain. Nothing happened between us—nothing could have happened between us. Yet something just kept you front and centre in my mind, and I haven't been able to let go. When I saw you last night, it was like a fuse was lit within me. Everything fell into place. I'm where I'm meant to be. But you're still untouchable."

I let out the breath I've been holding. I am unable to move, unable to talk. I've known Thomas for years, yet I don't know him well at all. I've spent so little time with Jack, yet I feel as though I've known him a lifetime. Still, it was like he said, I was unavailable. And I didn't want any more complications in my life.

"Olivia," he says, concern in his eyes when I start gasping for breath.

"I'm okay. I just forgot my water bottle."

"I've taken up enough of your time," he says, standing and extending his hand to help me up. I stand facing him, a million unsaid words passing between us.

"We'll meet again," he starts. "I have no doubt." And he turns away and walks out of my life.

CHAPTER 21

JACK

Morgan clings to me like a second skin. And all I want her to do is leave. I know she's looking for a man to latch on to, possibly husband material, but that man definitely isn't me. The fuck was mediocre at best, and now I'm second guessing having brought her back to my place, because she's angling for a key. Morgan is a woman I've known for years, a casual hook up because I'd rather not deal with hookers. But now she's trying to sink her teeth into me, and I can't seem to shake her off.

I send an SOS to Selena, who knows me well enough to realize exactly what I need. Five minutes later, my phone is ringing non-stop and I deliberately don't answer it, pretending I'm too invested in what Morgan has to say.

"Aren't you going to get that?" she asks, batting her eyes at the incessant ringing, irritated that I haven't put the device on silent.

"Oh," and I feign deafness. I pick up my phone as an alert comes through, frown, then tell her I have an urgent work matter that's come up. I stand, pocketing my phone.

"But I'm flying out tonight," she whines, and I realize I've never noticed just how whiney she is.

"This can't wait." I look at her regretfully, kiss the top of her forehead, and tell her to show herself out. I'm met with a blank stare, which I pretend not to notice, before I turn and head for the front door. I ignore the words she calls after me about being back in town next week and make a mental note to be unavailable for the next two weeks. Perhaps even the next year.

"When are you going to find yourself a decent girl and settle down?" Selena asks, when she answers my call.

"Make sure you make me unavailable for Morgan Creed when she calls the office," I tell her.

"For how long?"

"The term of her natural life. And are you offering?"

"Offering...?" I can just imagine Selena's puzzled look through the phone.

"You asked me when I was going to settle down. Are you offering?"

Selena laughs and tells me I'm too much of a man-whore for her tastes. The thing about Selena is that there is an easy relationship between us. She's worked for me for years, and we've become so comfortable with one another that she feels she can treat and talk to me like an older brother, and I in kind feel like she's the baby sister I never had and always wanted.

"Remind me again why I'm such a loser when it comes to women," I sigh, scrubbing a hand down my face. I feel like I'm getting too old for this shit. There's got to be more to life than this.

"You don't value yourself enough, Jack. You don't believe you have anything of substance to offer a long-term relationship, so you run away from women who pose a threat to your bachelorhood."

"I asked for a PA; I got a therapist instead," I mutter.

"Your Friday afternoon is confirmed with Ainsley Winmore," she tells me. "Will you require accommodation? Or will you be coming back to the city?"

"Set me up somewhere, Sel. I might make a weekend of it, see some other properties while I'm out there."

◆ ◆ ◆

Like all great bachelors, I have always harbored ambitions to remain in eternal bachelorhood. Realistically speaking, I knew that everything must eventually come to an end. I knew that one day, I would have to change my ways. Although I had quite hoped that day would come when I was somewhere in my sixties and close to my deathbed.

Instead, I find myself thinking more and more about the substance of my life. I'm still thirsty to conquer the business world and drag down as many unsuspecting competitors as possible. But now I get an image of myself doing things I never would have done previously. I consider all the things I could do with my life that would offer some measure of reward.

I think about having a home, rather than a house. I want to sail around the world, but not without a companion. I want to have a warm body to come home to at night. And I want the pitter patter of tiny feet to run head on into me as I open the front door and enter my home at the end of a long day at work. I want all the creature comforts that I had never before considered or even imagined possible in my world. And all this was because of Olivia.

Olivia has managed to infiltrate my soul. She has cut me down and burrowed deep into my heart, building a home there for herself. She is the only woman I want to do all these things with. She is the first and the last. The only.

I can't seem to get her out of my mind, and things only get worse when I get to the office and Selena ignores me as I sidle past her desk. Her head is buried in her phone and she has the volume on loudspeaker as she watches what appears to be a news report. I regard her with a certain level of curiosity; Selena isn't usually invested in her phone, and she hates the news, so I wonder what's gotten her undivided attention.

"Selena?" I have to say her name twice before she looks up in surprise. She fumbles with her phone, then drops it, her face awash in guilt.

"Sorry, boss, I didn't see you there."

"What's wrong?"

She shakes her head, telling me whatever it is, she doesn't want to talk about it. She lowers her eyes to her desk and shuffles some documents on her desk, making herself appear productive. But I would know that look anywhere. Selena is hiding something from me.

"Out with it," I sigh.

When she shakes her head again, my reaction tells her I'm more than serious, and she swallows thickly before she relents. She picks up her phone and turns the screen towards me. There's a picture of Olivia and Thomas torn down the middle, with a blurb that states "Trouble in Paradise?" I don't keep up with the gossip columns past something inadvertently coming up on one of my feeds, so I have no idea what's going on with Olivia. I turn questioning eyes toward Selena; she would know.

"What's going on?" I ask her.

She shrugs and throws her arms up in the air. "Something about an argument at a charity ball. People are placing bets on how much longer they'll last."

"And?"

"Most people think she's too good for him. He's a cocky, handsome bastard, but Olivia seems to be extraordinarily high on the likability scale. More so than he is."

I scoff. "Would you look at that. He's the one that's whoring her out to the world for his own gain, but the world seems to love her more than they'll ever like him."

CHAPTER 22

OLIVIA

I'm finishing up a meeting when Thomas pops his head into the office unexpectedly to take me out to lunch. He walks straight into a meeting I'm having with Teddy, one of our chief designers. There's something seriously wrong with him, because he seems agitated as he wordlessly crosses my office and starts to pummel Teddy. The young man barely scrapes past Thomas as he flees the room. I'm dumbstruck at the attack, both unprovoked and unacceptable. Thomas leans over, breathing heavily, and I stand from behind my desk, every bone in my body trembling with anger. I'm humiliated beyond words that he's come into my workplace and done this.

"What the hell has gotten into you?" I hiss.

"Don't you dare turn this around on me, Olivia."

"How dare you! How dare you come into my place of business and act this way. What is wrong with you?"

When Amy comes running into the room, she closes the door behind her and straightens her back. I don't even know what to say to her.

"What's going on here?" she asks.

Thomas points a menacing finger in her direction and snarls at her.

"You have no right to barge in here without so much as a knock, nor involve yourself in business which is none of your concern."

Amy looks at me, taking in my state. I'm visibly shaken, possibly in shock. Thomas did that; Thomas reduced me to this anxious wreck. Amy's cool and calm as she looks at me, then starts talking directly to Thomas. I can see there is so much she wants to say, but she focuses only on getting the resolution she requires.

"I want you to step away from the desk and leave this building now, otherwise I will have you forcibly removed," she tells him.

"Why, you..." And with that, Thomas lunges at Amy, but she simply sidesteps, and he goes crashing into a nearby chair just as two burly security guards come running into the office.

I watch as they grab Thomas by his arms, physically restraining him as he tries to argue his way out of the situation. The security guards look to me for direction, but I only shake my head and tell them to take him out of the building. I'm too shaken to direct any words at Thomas, but it is at this point that I understand something I was blind to the past few weeks. Thomas has gone over the edge, and there's no coming back for us.

♦ ♦ ♦

At Amy's insistence, I leave the city and drive to my father's home in the Hamptons. She seems to think it would be a good idea for me to get away and the house my father owns in Sag Harbor is the one place where Thomas and I don't have any memories, so he wouldn't know where to find me, even if he tried. My father has somehow got wind of the disaster that unfolded at work today and calls me as I roll through the traffic late on Friday afternoon. It takes a while to convince him that I'm okay, and he agrees that my getting away is for the best.

When Ainsley calls me a mere few minutes later, I know it's my father who's informed her of the situation and my whereabouts. Ainsley tells me she herself is in the Hamptons for the weekend, and insists I drop by her house to debrief before I head to my own home for the night. I don't know how I'm going to explain the situation to Ainsley. Thomas has done so much damage to me mentally, I feel I've become a fragile mess ready to collapse in on myself. He embarrassed me at the Charity Ball, and then he came into my work and assaulted a fellow colleague. Without warning. For no apparent reason. Thomas was obviously hanging on by a thread. And there was no longer a place for him in my life.

I weave my way through Sag Harbor, glad for the respite of lazy traffic and quaint, sleepy towns. "Just what I need," I murmur, as I come to a stop at the end of the winding driveway to Ainsley's beach house. I catch my breath as I look up at the property and admire its beauty; the house never ceased to amaze me every time I saw it. It was a rare gem of a Colonial, steepled on a slight hill that led directly to the water's edge, taking up a half an acre block and towering majestically over perfectly manicured grounds.

Ainsley throws the front door open even before I reach it. "Well, finally!" she squeals grabbing my forearm and ushering me into the house. "I thought you'd never get here! Come, come."

I don't even have a chance to say hello in between Ainsley's ramblings about having waited for me for hours. I look at the eccentric old lady with her silver pink hair and bite back a bemused laugh.

"Ainsley, we only spoke an hour ago," I remind her. "You haven't been waiting that long. And you know how traffic is on a Friday night."

"Yes, yes," Ainsley agrees, stretching to stand at her full height.

"You know, you can always admit that you miss me," I laugh.

Ainsley scoffs and waves me away. I know she missed me the few days she's been away from the office. Ainsley, who hasn't had any children of her own, has always treated me as though I am her own flesh and blood.

"I had Mabel prepare a spread for afternoon tea before she left for the day," Ainsley says, leading me into the great room. From what I understand, it is the only inhabitable room in the house at the moment— that, the kitchen, and one bathroom are all that remain. I take inhabitable to mean the only room with four walls standing and a makeshift table and chairs. Every other piece of furniture has been moved into storage while the renovations are underway. Ainsley has totally stripped the house and is knocking down walls and refinishing the entire internal shell. And although the house in the Hamptons is only a holiday home, she insists it be done to the highest standards.

"So let me show you what we've done so far," Ainsley suggests, moving to lead me from room to room to show me the debris of what had been a perfectly good home, but now stood as an empty shell of the past. "And here," she explains, coming into what had once been the informal dining room off the kitchen, "I plan to knock down this wall... oh, there you are!"

Ainsley startles as she comes across a man at the kitchen sink, washing his hands. The man, himself startled, turns to look at us, and I gasp and take a step back when I see Jack Speed standing there. An awkward, deathly silence falls upon the room, as Ainsley looks from me to him but says nothing.

Finally, Jack smiles and moves toward me, wiping his wet hands against his jeans.

"What the hell is wrong with you two?" Ainsley asks. She tsks and shakes her head as she looks at us both, then sighs and looks down at her watch. "Oh, dear, is that the time? We must have afternoon tea—yes, it's time for afternoon tea," she says. "Come, children," she prompts, her voice stern enough for Jack and me to look at each other and realize she means us. She's reduced us to children.

We follow her to the great room and she takes her place at the head of the small table after she pours tea and advises us to fill our plates with the delicacies she's prepared.

"Why are we here?" I ask her, and I think I'm shell-shocked.

Ainsley ignores my question. "Lots of wonderful eateries in the area for dinner—but this should keep you going til then," she says, spreading jam onto her scone. She takes a bite, then sets it down on her plate. Jack and I look at her eagerly—I'm not sure why exactly we're enthralled by her every move and confused at the same time as to what we are both doing here. What were the chances that this was a coincidence?

Ainsley looks up at us as we watch her, her eyes cloudy as she frowns at us. "Go on, eat," she cajoles. "Eat." After a minute, half-way through buttering the other half of her scone, Ainsley lets the butter knife slide to her plate and curses under her breath. "Shoot. You know, I forgot, I have a standing appointment in town. I totally forgot about it. Maybe if I leave now, I can still make it," she says, rising from the table.

"I'll drive you," I offer, rising also.

"No, no, I have my car. You kids enjoy your afternoon tea—Jack can show you around once you're done eating." And with a flourish, Ainsley leaves the house and drives away, leaving us staring at one another awkwardly as we sit at the table.

"This is so bizarre." I give Jack a tight smile.

"Oh, you have no idea," Jack agrees, grinning at me.

I look down at my plate uncomfortably. I hate that I've been put in this position. Especially now when my emotions are all over the place after what happened with Thomas today. I have a feeling that Ainsley has orchestrated the whole situation this afternoon, although I don't see how she possibly would have known I'd be coming to the Hamptons, since the trip was very last minute.

"If it's any consolation," Jack begins, "I didn't know you'd be here."

"I didn't know you'd be here. Why are you here, Jack?" I ask him.

Jack laughs. "Ainsley mentioned she's putting this house on the market and she wanted me to have a look before anyone else. She knows I'm looking for a home here."

"This house? She wants to sell this house?" I look at him incredulously.

"That's what she said."

"You have got to be kidding me," I mutter, more for my own benefit than his. "I don't know why she roped you into coming here, but there's no way Ainsley would ever sell this house, Jack. You're wasting your time here."

"I don't consider this a waste of time, Olivia."

He gives me a wistful look. This is personal for him. More than looking at a house he's interested in purchasing, his objective is that he finally got me in a position where there'll be no escape for me.

"Do you think she set this whole thing up?" I ask him.

"Oh, you can bet your bottom dollar she did. She's a sly one, that boss of yours."

"But she didn't know I'd be coming out here today," I argue. "This was very much a last-minute trip on my part."

"That's something to consider. She set this meeting up with me last week, so that's something."

♦ ♦ ♦

We fell into effortless conversation. Where it had at first been awkward and stiff sitting opposite one another, now our resolve had calmed and we spoke as though we were old friends bumping into each other after a brief interlude apart. It was so easy to put Thomas to the back of my mind in the company of Jack.

"Ainsley has a beautiful home," he remarks, lifting his eyes to survey the twelve-foot ceilings. "I'd definitely buy it if she wants to sell."

"It is a beautiful place. And the view doesn't hurt, either," I laugh. "But I'm telling you now, she won't sell. That was her excuse to get you out here for some reason."

"You seem to know her so well."

"She's been the one constant in my life since my birth," I tell him.

"So you guys go way back," he exclaims. "So now I understand the influence she's had over your creative genius."

"That's definitely all Ainsley. She's been a very positive role model for me."

"Where did you just go?" Jack asks, when I get so carried away with thoughts of the past that I sit in a daze for a few moments, looking out the window wistfully. I snap out of my reverie and look at him, taking in his features, and the cloud moving across his piercing blue eyes. Amy had been right—Jack is devastatingly handsome.

"It's getting late," Jack says finally. "I wouldn't want you driving back to New York too late at night."

I shake my head slightly, confused, but say nothing. I turn to look out the bay window, deep in contemplation for a moment. I had come to the Hamptons to spend the weekend alone, to think and contemplate the next steps in my relationship with Thomas. I was glad Amy had decided not to come along; this weekend would give me a chance to do some soul-searching and finally create the canvas for my future. Nothing was going to change that. And no matter what I chose to do, or how I decided to steer my life, no one was going to influence my decision, no matter what.

I looked back at Jack, still staring at me, and saw a dynamic yet enigmatic man. I saw in him raw passion in everything he did, stability and strength. All the things I desired. But what I also saw was a complication.

CHAPTER 23

OLIVIA

"Jack is under the impression that you drove back to New York last night," Ainsley tells me. I step back from the doorway and let her into the house.

"There's no reason for him to believe otherwise, Ainsley."

Ainsley shoots me a 'why not?' as she walks through the house. She reaches the large glass sliding door that leads out to the porch overlooking the beach and takes a seat before I have a chance to invite her to do so.

"Ainsley, what's going on?" I ask finally, without taking a seat.

Ainsley picks up the book that I had set down and surveys the cover. I knows she's already read the book, because I saw it in her office on a few occasions. But instead of telling me this, she asks me if the book is any good.

I shrug. "It's good."

"Dear child, always so serious. Come, sit," she says tapping the seat beside her. Ainsley regards me thoughtfully, then squeezes my hand in her own, setting it on her knee.

"The reason I was so adamant you come to see me yesterday was so I'd ensure you'd end up staying the weekend rather than driving back down. You've been so unhappy for a while now; I thought the time up here could give you some clarity. I was not trying to set you up with Jack."

"I know you invited him up last week. There's no way you could have known I'd be coming up this weekend."

I absolve her of any guilt she may feel and lean against the railing, crossing my feet at the ankles.

"I thought you two had buried your differences."

"It was a working relationship, Ainsley. You may not have set up this weekend, but I know what you're thinking."

"What's wrong with being friends?" Ainsley asks innocently.

"Nothing. Absolutely nothing. But Jack is a complication I can do without right now."

"You mean he'd complicate things between you and Thomas?"

"I'm leaving Thomas. I don't want to give anyone a reason to blame the breakup on a third party. Which is exactly where the gossip mongers will go. You know that."

Ainsley rises from her seat and walks towards the rails. She pauses then lays her hands upon the frame, looking out at the sea. For the longest time, she says nothing, merely stands staring out at the beach as the waves crash against the rocks in the distance.

"I want to share something with you, Olivia. Something I have never shared with anyone before. Then you do what you need to do." She sighs heavily, and I can see her knuckles are white where she squeezes the metal too hard. "When I was twenty-two, I was madly in love with a man. A man of means, but by no measure as wealthy as my parents desired him to be. You know, I grew up with privilege, and I was expected to marry even further up. This man was about twelve rungs down. Needless to say, my mother's constant meddling ensured I ended up married to a Vanderbilt instead. Money, prestige, power... all the things my family desired. Yet, my heart was not in it. Even though I married a good man, he was not the man I was in love with. With my one true love, there had been a certain magic... an incomprehensible energy in the room anytime we were together. That buzz, that passion—I never felt it ever again until I ran into him again twenty-five years later. We happened to attend the same function, and we ran into each other. That room was abuzz with that energy; it was still there. I tend to believe we were true soulmates."

I shake my head slightly, not understanding the point of her story. "Why are you telling me this?" Ainsley has a pained look on her face.

"I'm fifty-three years old, Olivia. I've been married three times, but never once have I felt that passion with any one of my husbands. I haven't felt that chemistry since I was twenty-two. Until you walked into my home with Jack. And when you walked into that room yesterday, the air was filled with electricity when you two saw each other. My point is, sometimes the thing you've been looking for your whole life is the one thing you can't see when it's standing right there in front of you."

◆ ◆ ◆

When Ainsley leaves, I stand at the window and watch as the waves pull closer into the shore, kicking up sand and seaweed as the swell pushes back out to the sea. Ainsley did a really good job of messing with my head. Maybe not intentionally, but she did so nonetheless, because everything she said was spot on. I was not immune to the magic between Jack and me. The air was palpable with passion any time we were in a room together, and there was no disguising the chemistry between us, no matter how hard I tried to fight it.

I sighed and moved away from the window. I had pretty much made up my mind on the drive on Friday night that Thomas and I could no longer continue on with one another. No matter how much it hurt to let him go after more than two years together, I could so clearly see that our relationship had run out of steam. But by the same token, I couldn't complicate the situation with thoughts of another man. Jack was everything I needed, but the timing was off. Which made us wrong for one another on so many levels.

I brushed my fingers against the curve of the sofa, lost in my own world as I walked through the living room. I traversed from room to room, my cluttered thoughts my only ally. I couldn't deny the feelings brewing between Jack and me. But there was no reason we couldn't at least be friends.

CHAPTER 24

JACK

"I thought you'd gone back to the city," I tell her, sliding into the empty chair opposite Olivia.

When she'd left me last night, she hadn't indicated she was staying the weekend in the Hamptons. Her call mid-morning not only took me by surprise, but it was a welcome reprieve from the house-hopping I'd been doing this morning in search of properties.

"I decided to stay," she tells me.

She's wearing jeans and a gorgeous green top tucked in at the waist, which is doing illegal things to my mind. I raise my hand for the barista and place our coffee order.

"You sure you don't want something to eat?" I ask her.

"Thank you. Coffee is my liquid gold."

She smiles at me then looks around the quaint little cafe. Like all cafes this side of town, it is bustling with patrons both sitting and lining up for take-away. I can't stop looking at her. And I can't believe she called and asked me if I wanted to go for coffee.

"So why did you come to the Hamptons this weekend?" I ask her. "You said it was a spur of the moment decision."

She sucks in her cheeks and plays with her cup of coffee before raising it to her lips.

"You could say I'm running away," she says, finally lifting her eyes to mine.

"From what?"

She shrugs. She wants to share, but she has a hard time knowing where to start.

"Life. Work. Relationships. They've all crossed over into each other, so the lines are blurry right now."

"Things can get that way sometimes," I muse. If I can take away at least some of her burdens, I'd be more than happy to.

"Perhaps. But probably not for someone like you," she tells me. "You're so well put together, you probably don't need to worry about human frailty."

This earns her a laugh from me. I do understand that at times, things may be harder for women. They're more emotionally invested in things, and more vulnerable.

"I have my challenges," I remind her. "They might not look like yours, but they're still burdens."

"I'm breaking off my engagement," she blurts out suddenly. This is news to me. Not entirely unwelcome news, but it's news nonetheless. I want to do little happy laps around the cafe, but I don't want to appear insensitive. I understand she's told me because she probably just wants me to listen. She doesn't need me to tell her what a bum her fiancé is or that she's better off without him. No. She needs me to just be her rock today. And I can fill those shoes for her.

"You're upset," I surmise. She seems taken by surprise that I've decided to validate her feelings rather than tell her she should never have gotten engaged to him in the first place. Not that she did, as I understand it. Apparently, he sprung the engagement on her knowing she would have to go along with it to save face.

"I am upset. But it has to happen. I just don't know what he's capable of."

"You think he would try to hurt you?"

I had never considered that Thomas could become so volatile that he could physically hurt her.

"He attacked one of my colleagues. Out of the blue. Without provocation."

"Is this why you came here?"

"I came here to think. To get away from him and clear my head. I just couldn't be where he is any longer. And he just kept flooding my phone with texts and calls."

"And he's not doing that now?" I ask her.

"He is." She gives me a cheeky grin. "But I've switched my phone off. There's no danger of him turning up here because I'm not answering his calls."

I give her a long thoughtful look as I digest more insight into the nature of their relationship. It's not a good one. And someone like Olivia should never have been with someone like Thomas Thackeray.

"I think you need to do what's right for you."

Olivia nods her head in understanding, giving me a grateful smile. I wish I could do more for her, but she tells me she'd like to change the subject. She wants to relax and unwind this weekend, not waste any unspent energy on Thomas.

Our conversation turns to work, and we exchange details of all the projects we each have coming up.

"Do you think you'll have time to handle a hotel renovation I have coming up?" I ask her, looking at her face for any signs of interest.

"Ooh," she swoons, rubbing her palms together in excitement. "Hotel renovations are my favorite!"

"I've got the sketches right here," I tell her, grabbing the tube from the bag next to me. And with that, she moves our coffees to the side of the table as I open the tube of sketches, unfurling them on the table.

For the next hour, we discuss the sketches, measurements and interiors, and I listen intently as she makes some suggestions for little changes that would allow the work to flow better.

"At what stage would you want to meet again to go over the prelims?" she asks.

"Probably not until after the demolition." I consult my watch then roll the sketches up, inserting them back into the tube. "I'm flying out to Cali in a couple of days, so if you have any questions after that, it will have to be via teleconference or email. I'll discuss the mechanics with Ainsley."

"She doesn't know?"

"When I asked her, you were unavailable. I did specifically ask for you because of your fantastic work on the Goldsborough."

"You're not staying for the demolition?" She seems a little disappointed. Or maybe that's just my imagination.

"No need. It's pretty straight forward."

For a moment, I feel a pinch in my heart. I don't want to leave, but my base is in California. That's where the majority of my work is, and I've been away long enough; there are issues there which require my attention.

"Something wrong?" I ask, noting the deflated look on her face.

She shakes her head and looks up at the crowded line that is waiting to be served at the counter. "It's the simple things," she tells me. "The most basic and simple things, like lining up for coffee, is what I crave most in my life."

CHAPTER 25

OLIVIA

Why complicate things with extra baggage that is not required? This is what I'm thinking as I sit at the small table with Jack, drinking my coffee. I can't understand what possessed me to call him and ask him to have coffee with me. As we chat, he doesn't judge me or remind me that Thomas isn't the right man for me. Instead, he just lets me talk, listening patiently and offering small pearls of wisdom where anyone else would have given the kind of unsolicited advice that I can definitely do without.

"I'll call you if I need to follow up on anything," I tell him, standing up suddenly and collecting my coat from the chair beside me. Jack is watching me carefully, almost as if he's expecting me to say something, but he remains silent as I fling the coat across my arm and smile down at him. There are unspoken words in his eyes, but for whatever reason, he holds them in as I thank him for the coffee and wish him a safe flight.

My phone rings just as I'm about to walk away; fumbling with my coat, I reach into my handbag and retrieve it, pulling it out to see a blocked number. There is no answer to my greeting, only the deep breathing of someone on the line as I repeatedly ask who's calling. I look down at Jack, who watches me inquisitively, then hang up the phone in exasperation.

"Does that happen often?" he asks.

"Not often enough for me to be concerned about," I smile. "I hope you have a safe trip, Jack. I'll see you when I see you."

"I'll be here until tomorrow night if you want to catch up again," he says, and I give him a tight smile. Why complicate an already complicated situation? The first step is for me to rid myself of Thomas before anything else. I can't even start to think about anyone or anything else until that is done and dusted.

"Let's play it by ear." And with that, I turn on my heels and exit the cafe, putting a safe distance between myself and Jack Speed.

◆ ◆ ◆

When I decide to cook myself a meal, I don't take into account that the kitchen hasn't been used in a while. Even though I'm all alone and the smart thing is to order in, I decide instead to cook, and end up with a disaster on my hands. A disaster which I have no idea how to navigate.

It's a Saturday night and my kitchen sink has

sprung a leak. And by leak, I mean the tap is gushing like Niagara Falls and I can't seem to get the faucet shut. I can't even minimize the amount of water splashing back at me from the sink. The only number I have for a local plumber isn't answering, and the sink, quickly filling, is starting to overflow, with the water leaking over the lip of the kitchen bench and onto the hardwood floors. The damage this water could cause gives me heart palpitations.

I grab my phone again and lift it to my ear, considering the only option I have. I call Jack and explain the situation to him. I pause so he can move past his laughter and rattle off my address, leaving him with a promise to come and assist. I throw towels on the floor to stem the rush of water as it continues to gush and flow, fumbling with the faucet again. I only manage to make the water gush harder and I step back, deciding to wait for Jack instead.

"You didn't tell me you were a klutz in the kitchen also," he jokes, when he arrives with a plumber in tow. I don't know where he found him on such short notice, but I've never been more grateful as I am when he manages to get the water under control and tells me I'll need a new faucet. He leaves with a promise to come back and install one the next morning.

"So... no thank you drink?" Jack asks, once the plumber is gone and we're standing in the doorway watching him drive off.

"I think the whole house needs a renovation," I mutter, ignoring his question and looking around at the house. I have to avoid looking at his hypnotizing blue eyes or I'll fall into an abyss from which there's no return.

"Could be," he murmurs. "I know a great designer."

The look he gives me destroys my heart and leaves me breathless. No one has ever looked at me with such a sense of longing. No one but him.

Jack, who could disappear from my life then re-emerge and make it seem like he had been there all along. Jack, who was handsome when I'd met him months ago, but now melts my heart. Jack, who would only get better with time.

I don't realize I'm staring, lost in his eyes, until he moves forward and crowds me. He lifts a hand to my cheek and rubs his thumb back and forth, his attention focused on me. There is yearning in his eyes, a longing I'm not accustomed to. My own fiancé doesn't even look at me that way, and I catch my breath in anticipation of what's to come. My hand goes up to meet his against my cheek as we stand silently doing an awkward dance around one another. There is so much want between us. We want so much. We crave so much. I have never felt such a strong attraction to any man. I have never so much as looked at another man since Thomas and I got together, but this is one man I cannot clear from my head. There he resides, dwelling in that deep dark recess where thought and logic live.

I can't help myself any more than he can. My body moves of its own accord, pressing into him as my lips crash against his and we kiss. A long, lingering caress that sucks the life out of me. He takes my breath away. He jars my soul. And he claims my heart.

"I can't," I say, pulling away. "I can't do this to Thomas."

"I thought you said it was over?"

"It is. I haven't told him yet."

"But you will?"

He wants confirmation. He wants to know that it's ending with Thomas and starting with us.

"I'll tell him when I get back to New York. I have to do this in person."

"And what of us?" he asks me.

"Then, and only then, will I call you."

CHAPTER 26
OLIVIA

Thomas has never asked me to move into his place. And I appreciate my privacy, so I never asked him to move in with me either. Instead, we kept our respective residences on different sides of town, respecting each other's space as we went about our own lives. Even after we were engaged. We did however have keys we exchanged at some point in time, for the rare occasions when we picked up each other's laundry or other items that needed to be dropped off.

I put the key into the door and enter Thomas's apartment, closing the door behind me. Today is the day that I would break the news of our engagement to him. This couldn't be done in a public place; I could offer him that one concession. I would also give him his key back. And we would have a conversation, like normal adults, about how to break the news to the world.

I am no longer concerned about how a broken engagement will affect my father after his recent legal battles. If anything, my father is pushing for the breakup, and has made it more than clear that I am his priority, not the way the public perceives him, regardless of what that would cost him. Today will be the day. I will disengage myself from Thomas and then go on with the rest of my life. This could no longer wait.

I set my keys down on the kitchen bench, noticing a set of keys and a wallet on the countertop by the sink. Both look unfamiliar, and as I contemplate reaching over to check the identification of the wallet owner, I hear a low murmur, followed by a moan. I stand still, the hairs on the back of my neck standing, rooted to the spot in silence, then take a step backwards out of the kitchen.

A million thoughts race through my head as I move slowly down the hallway. I wonder if Thomas has loaned his apartment to one of his friends, even knowing that this would be so unlike him. He is almost obsessive about cleanliness and would never hand over his keys to someone who would not treat his home with the same respect he does.

I round the corner just as another moan fills the air. For some reason, the only thought that has not run through my mind as I made my way through the apartment is that Thomas would actually be at home in the middle of the day, and that he would have company. This is the farthest thing from my mind as I reach the bedroom and stand in the doorway surveying the scene.

I stand facing the bed, shock invading all my senses as I stare straight at Thomas's face as he rams into a man crouched on all fours. Of all the things I could have imagined finding here today, this is not what I was expecting. I don't know what makes me angrier—the betrayal of Thomas cheating on me or the fact that he kept his sexual orientation a closely guarded secret. I did not see this one coming.

Thomas sees me just as I register the scene, and his face contorts with dueling emotions; pain that I am standing there and now I know, and pleasure as he reaches his orgasm with one final punishing thrust. His mouth drops into a silent 'O' and his face pales as the magnitude of what's happening registers. I hear him scream my name as I turn to walk away. I stumble through the apartment and grab my keys as I make my way to the front door, where Thomas catches up to me. He is drenched in sweat, his dick still hard as it slaps against his thighs. He grabs my arm and pulls me back, trying to hold on to me as I struggle to push away from him.

"Olivia, wait..." he pleads.

"Get away from me," I scream, trying to get past him.

"Just wait. I have to explain. Please, Olivia."

I have never seen him so contrite. And I have never been as angry as I am right now.

"You disgust me. Get your hands off me!"

"No. Just stay. Olivia, I swear to you, just let me explain."

"What's to explain, Thomas? What's to explain?" I yell at him, slapping him repeatedly across the chest.

The other man comes running down the hallway, half-clothed, heading for the door, in a hurry to get out of the apartment. I don't know who he is. I gasp, startled, as he storms past me and leaves. I try to follow, but Thomas holds onto me tightly and pulls me back into the apartment.

"You're not going anywhere, Olivia. Not until we talk."

He's trying to control the narrative of our lives again, and this just makes me that much angrier.

"There's nothing to talk about," I yell. "There will be no wedding. There is no 'us'. Now get out of my way so I can leave." I am near hysterical as I flail about in distress.

Thomas is furious when he looks at me, and I can feel the moment that he is about to blow a fuse. He reaches his hand back and lets it fall to my cheek, sending me hurtling into the wall, where I hit my head painfully and slide to the ground.

I shake the dizziness from my head and look up at a naked Thomas, who is now headed for the liquor cabinet. There are so many emotions running through me as I rear my head in surprise. This is a whole other side of him I have never seen before. I had thought that by coming here and rationalizing my decision for us to break up in private, everything would go smoothly. Never did I consider that he could get violent or crazy or do any of the things that he is now doing.

My cheek stings, smarting from the slap he's dealt me. Thomas drinks straight from the bottle as he watches me struggle to lift myself off the floor. His dick has gone limp, and as I rise slowly, putting a shaking hand to my throbbing head, he starts to stroke himself, reaching a full erection almost within seconds. Discarding the bottle, he lunges at me and catches me off guard, locking my arms in front of me.

"You interrupted my afternoon siesta," Thomas hisses. "But that's okay, we can make up for it together." My eyes flutter open and I watch in horror as he unzips my pants and attempts to roll them down my thighs. I try in vain to fight him off. Before I have a chance to scream, his hand flies to my mouth and I'm rendered helpless yet again. "Scream and this won't end well, Olivia," he warns, as he rips my blouse open. I squirm under his touch, struggling in vain as he stares down at me with inhuman eyes. Something inside him has snapped, and I'm afraid of what's to come. I can't believe this is happening.

"Don't, Thomas. Please. Don't," I beg, as his hand moves from my mouth to my neck. He grabs me harshly, almost cutting off my circulation, until I find myself sputtering, unable to scream or fight him off as he attacks me. I feel his erection as it meanders between my thighs, and look at him, wondering how far he could possibly take this. There's no mistaking the fear that is causing my heart to beat out of my chest. I try to shake him free of my throat, but the more I fight him, the more excited he gets.

I know. I know in that moment what is going to happen. And after that, he will probably kill me. I can't believe it, don't want to believe it, but deep inside, I know what is coming. I close my eyes and pray that it will be quick. I feel sick inside, like someone has scraped my insides out. My blood is curdling. My skin is crawling.

"This is how it's going to be forever, Olivia," Thomas says, his hand around my neck. "It will be me or nothing at all for you." Again, that piercing hiss as his breath weaves across my face. He laughs; a deep, evil, belly aching laugh. I feel revolted, dirty and violated as he tries to ram his cock into me. He is in such an excited frenzy that he misses the mark and looks down, momentarily loosening his grip on my neck. "You're... mine," he breathes. I follow his eyes down toward his dick, which has started to deflate, and inhale a sharp breath. His eyes are now focused on one thing more than they are on me. If I don't do something now, I know I won't leave this apartment alive.

My keys have fallen to the ground. With the only strength I have left, I slide my foot around Thomas's and send us both hurtling to the ground together. He tightens his arms around me, but not before I am able to reach the keys and bring them up, swinging my hand across his face.

"Bitch!" He hisses, his punishing hands falling away from my body. I scramble to my feet, almost tripping over the jeans around my legs. I lift them quickly, fumble with the door, then take flight, Thomas's whimpers of pain following me down the hall as I put distance between us. I'm sore and torn from the inside out, but my legs keep moving. An inner voice tells me to burn the place to the ground. I wonder where to go and what to do, think of my father and the devastation that something like this will cause him. He can't know. No, I will never tell him. I can't. I will just get rid of Thomas and go on with my life; there was no need for any further destruction. I burst through the revolving doors of the building, register the shock on the doorman's face as I hold my torn blouse together, then start to run toward an uncertain future that will deal with the past in its own uncertain way.

CHAPTER 27

JACK

Olivia won't take my calls. I call her several times but each and every call has gone unanswered. Ever since we came back to New York, I haven't been able to reach her. I find myself taking to social media for any news about her broken engagement but find nothing. Even Thomas, usually so vocal on media platforms, seems to have gone to ground, and I can't read the situation as it is without a thread from Olivia.

I'm heading back to California when I ask Marcus to divert and head to Olivia's office. I know she's not there, because Selena has done some digging and knows she hasn't been going in to work. Ainsley however, is there and she could be my last salvation for contacting Olivia.

As always, Ainsley is the perfect host, and although I've turned up to her office unannounced, she welcomes me as I'm led into her office. I plant a kiss atop her head and fix her with a loving smile. This is the woman who I've come to learn has been like a mother to Olivia. She's been one of my closest confidantes for years, and she's also the woman who brought Olivia into my life. Knowing this, I don't understand how it is that I've never crossed paths with Olivia before.

I don't know where to begin. I take a seat and fold my long legs across one another. Ainsley says nothing but she knows exactly why I'm here. She's known me long enough to know when something's bothering me.

"Olivia's not here, Jack," she tells me, but she's not upset knowing I've come here for Olivia. If anything, I know she'd probably be the first to support a relationship between Olivia and me.

"I know that," I tell her.

"She's not in a good place, Jack. She needs time and space. I don't know when she'll be back."

"Tell me how I can help her."

Ainsley seems crushed. She's a woman who has faced adversity in her life. She has come back fighting each and every time. She has risen in the face of disaster and gone on to become bigger and better. But this thing with Olivia, whatever it is, has defeated her. She won't tell me what's happened, and I won't pry—that's as far as I'll go. But I just need to know that Olivia is okay.

"It's just going to take time," she tells me. "The fallout with Thomas was ugly. She's decided to take some time off and concentrate on her self-care."

"What aren't you telling me?" I ask, lowering my legs and rising to my full height. I walk toward her, coming to a stop near her desk, and turn concerned eyes towards her.

"Jack, I implore you. Olivia will call you when she's ready. I need you to respect her privacy and give her the space she needs to heal. She's no good to you in her current state."

"All this from a simple break up?"

"Nothing is ever simple with Thomas," she mutters, her voice scathing as she says his name.

I work my jaw, trying to keep my calm. She won't tell me what happened between them, and I'm not sure I want to know. The only thing I feel like doing right now is wringing Thomas's neck for any pain he's caused Olivia.

An overwhelming sense of loss consumes me as I leave the office, my pace quick as I slam my hand into the elevator before I get into it. And the last thing I see as I get in and the doors shut is Olivia's best friend Amy as she stands staring at me, a confused look on her face.

❖ ❖ ❖

I take the jet back to California and throw myself back into my work. I over-extended my stay in New York on this last trip, so there are multiple issues waiting for me to address. I attack the list that Selena has left me with a vengeance and a thirst for blood. I'm cut-throat when I'm angry, and this is one of those times when I'm not just angry but furious.

At 4pm, Luke Mitchell makes his entrance into my office, removes his cowboy hat and takes a seat across from me. The beauty of having someone like Luke on my team is that although he sticks out like a sore thumb, everyone trusts a cowboy. And trust is what Luke banks his success on. He's a private investigator I've used in the past and I trust him implicitly. Put simply, he's the best at what he does. I push the envelope across the table toward him but allow my hand to rest on it before he can pick it up.

"This is personal," I tell him. "I need full confidentiality."

"As always." When he smiles, there are two deep craters in his cheeks; dimples which seem to drive the lady's crazy. Like I said, everyone trusts a cowboy. But a baby-faced cowboy with dimples… they don't stand a chance.

"I want your best on this case and I want it done as soon as possible."

He opens the envelope, takes a cursory glance at the paper in his hand, then flicks his eyes in my direction without raising his head. There are questions in his glance, questions I don't want to get into, but he's obviously put together a picture of what's going on here. I'd rather he assumes that picture all on his own than for me to explain the situation to him.

"What am I looking for?" he asks me.

"Locations, first and foremost. Specifically if they're in the same time zone. Then history. Any dirt you can dig up on the male."

He nods in understanding and asks me about the timeline.

"I want this done yesterday," I tell him. He knows I'll pay anything he asks if I need something urgently, and he's never let me down thus far.

"I'll have something for you within twenty-four hours."

◆ ◆ ◆

At some point, I realize I start to wonder if the reason Olivia is avoiding me is because she and Thomas didn't actually break up. And Ainsley may have been trying to let me down easy. There has been nothing posted on social media and now both have dropped off the face of the earth. It could even have been that they have eloped and decided to keep the matter low key. I don't know Olivia's father Max well enough to contact him for confirmation, but I am determined to find out in my own way.

I know that when Olivia and I parted in Sag Harbor, she had been adamant that she and Thomas were over. Anything could have happened in the time between when I'd last seen her and when she met with Thomas. But I wasn't going to stand down and accept not knowing. I wasn't going to let her simply walk out of my life when I knew with everything in me that there was something brewing between us. It may have been sudden. And it may have been unexpected. But it was still us.

CHAPTER 28

OLIVIA

Hindsight is such a wonderful thing. The only downfall is that it usually rears its ugly head after the fact. After the spiral downward. After the pain and heartbreak of slowly waking up to realize that everything you'd built a life around was a lie...

I stumble out onto the street and hail the first taxi I can find. I fumble with my phone and call Amy, asking her to meet me at my house as soon as she can. I need to get home. I need to scrub Thomas off me and collect my thoughts. I need to make a change so drastic, it will shatter the carefully built bubble in which I have insulated myself.

The first thing I do once I'm home is grab a duffel bag and pack a few things in it. No sooner do I arrive back in New York from the Hamptons than I am planning to run away again.

My phone rings. I look down at the screen, see that it's Jack, and let it go to voicemail. I can't afford to stop and deal with him right now. I have to leave. I climb into the shower and scrub

Thomas off my skin. Then I collect the clothes I was wearing and stuff them into a garbage bag. It will be up to Amy to take them and destroy them before the memory of them destroys me.

I look in the mirror and I'm shocked at the flat gaze that stares back out at me. I feel so desolate and dirty, scratching at my skin like I can sear Thomas off my flesh. Nothing makes sense anymore, yet everything makes perfect sense. The signs I missed. The idiocy of going along with his stupid announcement that we were engaged. The warnings everyone threw me. All warnings and signs I chose to ignore.

Thomas really did do a number on me. He had me eating out of his hand the whole time we were together. If only I had been more on guard, but I suppose that's what he was so good at—knocking down my defenses.

I circle my own mind with self-loathing as I consider all the ways he's fooled me into thinking that he loves me. Thomas loves no one but himself. Everything that has ever happened between us was for his benefit. Our whole relationship had been based on a lie. I had merely been a vehicle for him to get where he wanted to go. So many situations where he was calculating the end game, and what he hoped to receive from a union with me. What hadn't been so obvious to me before was now so clear to see; I had been a tool he could use to further his station in society.

♦ ♦ ♦

"Any news?" I ask.

My oldest friend looks at me with weary, sympathetic eyes. "Nothing. No one's seen nor heard from him. He's literally disappeared."

"Do you think I'm over-reacting? Who else would be calling me just to breathe down the line?"

"Honey, maybe it's time we told your father?"

I look at Amy like she's lost her mind. She knows what my father is like. I'd already lost enough, and I didn't relish the possibility of losing my father over someone as insignificant as Thomas.

"You know he already suspects something is wrong," she points out.

"There's no way on this earth my father is going to find out what happened, Amy. You swore you wouldn't tell him."

"I won't," she rushes to explain. "But you're dealing with a psychopath here, Olivia. You need to understand that."

"We've already changed all the access codes at the offices and my home. Security has been stepped up. I feel safe, Amy. My lawyers will make it very clear to him that the engagement is off. He disappeared and didn't turn up to work so he lost his job. I don't think there's anything that would entice him to return to the city."

"I hope you're right, Olivia."

She doesn't seem convinced that Thomas has disappeared into the background quietly, but drops the matter, and I take this opportunity to tell her where my head is at.

"I've actually been thinking of going away for a while," I begin, regarding my friend solemnly.

"Maybe that's the best thing you could do for yourself right now."

"I need to get away from the city and concentrate on healing. I feel like I'm going mad here."

I force a tight smile then feel bad that I can't offer my best friend anything more.

"I think there's something you should know before you go," Amy tells me, and I turn to my friend. What more could there be for me to add to my overflowing basket of troubles?

"Jack Speed came by the office today."

This is not what I expected. He's been calling me incessantly for the past few days. I can't deal with him right now.

"And?"

I had told Amy about the kiss that Jack and I shared. I had gone into minute detail about every aspect of the moment, down to how it made me feel and how I was definitely looking forward to our next kiss. There had been no judgment from Amy's end. Instead, she'd been happy for me and told me it was about time I found someone who'd cherish me enough to want to spend every waking hour with me. Which had sent giddy butterflies up and down my veins.

"He wasn't in a good way, Olivia. I know you don't need this right now, but you should know. Selena's been calling the office daily. I guess he was concerned and decided to pay a visit instead."

"Did you speak with him?" I ask her.

She shakes her head and gives me a tight-lipped smile. "Ainsley did. He wanted to know why you weren't answering his calls. He left for California today. Selena doesn't seem to think he'll be back anytime soon."

She gives me a sympathetic look as I lower my head sadly, tears escaping the corners of my eyes. Just when I thought I was all cried out, my emotions got the better of me again. Thomas hadn't only destroyed us when he violated me. He'd destroyed me. And he'd destroyed any chance Jack and I had of a future together. My hatred for him grows as I think of all the things I've lost in the past few days. The tears come harsher and faster as I slump back against the sofa and hold a cushion to my face, burying my anguish in it. Nothing will ever be the same again.

CHAPTER 29

JACK

I look down at the file in front of me. I read the sheet again. Then again a third time. When I look back up, I ask Luke how sure he is of the information he's given me.

"I double checked myself," he tells me. "Everything is verified."

I'm in shock. Surprised, but glad. At least they're not together. Luke did a good job of locating Olivia and Thomas. And amazingly, they are on separate sides of the globe. Which I'm not too sure what that means, but I can only imagine the breakup was a bad one.

"She's definitely in Bali?" I ask.

"I've included the retreat she's staying in. It's a place for spiritual healing. I have one of my guys over there if you need to keep an eye on her," he offers.

"That won't be necessary."

Thomas is in Mexico. Slumming it in a room situated on top of a brothel, getting shit-faced day and night as he wallows in his own self-pity.

"Why is his background check empty?" I ask

Luke, looking up in surprise. I find it hard to believe that someone that's so active on social media doesn't have a few skeletons he'd like to keep safely locked away in his closet.

"It came back squeaky clean. Too clean, in fact. I have people doing a deep dive as we speak."

"He's hidden his tracks well," I point out.

"He must have some powerful friends to be able to do so," Luke tells me.

"He may know powerful people," I remind him, "but we *are* powerful people."

Now that I've got the information I asked for, I don't quite know what to do with it. I stand from my desk and go to stand at the window looking out at the valley. On a clear day, I can see forever, and that's why I love working from my home most days.

Olivia is in Bali. Alone. At a retreat. He must have really done a number on her for her to feel like she had to put distance between them. For a moment, I'm tempted to pick up the phone and have the jet fueled and waiting for me so I can fly to her. I stop myself though, realizing if she wanted me with her, she would have contacted me. She knows I've tried to, and I think she knows it's only a matter of time before we meet again. But this, I know, she has to do on her own. Whatever she's going through, she needs time and patience to sort through. And I'm a very patient man. I can wait for her forever if that's what's required of me.

◆ ◆ ◆

The danger for me being back in California is that I'm in close proximity to Morgan. She lives in California, and unfortunately, she knows where I live. Fortunately, my house is built like Fort Knox, so most days I'm able to keep her out by keeping my gates barricaded and not answering my phone, instead letting her know by text that I'm in meetings. It's a lie that usually flies, but there will come a time that it won't, and I don't look forward to that day.

I know I'm damaged beyond repair as the days pass without any word from Olivia and all I do is think about her day and night. She crosses my mind in that way that accidents happen that you never get over. I'm patient, but my patience is fraying, especially when I roll up to my home after a day of meetings and find Morgan leaning against the door of her red convertible. Suddenly, I'm reminded of all the things she's not and all the things that Olivia is. For one, she'd never parade around town in a chili-red convertible. She's caught me on my way in and now I'm forced to let her through the gates.

"Morgan," I greet her, my voice casual and uninviting. She climbs out of her car and attacks me even before I've closed my car door. She jumps at me and winds her long legs around my waist, clinging to me like a lost puppy.

"I've missed you sooo much," she coos, peppering my face with kisses. I peel her hands from around my neck and set her on her feet.

"I've been busy," I explain.

"Too busy even to call me back when you miss my calls?"

She pouts. Like actually pouts. I take in her blonde hair and blue eyes. Any other man would jump at a chance with her. Yet the more I look at her and have to sit through her conversation, the more I realize she'll never be anything to me other than a way to pass the time.

"You know I'm a busy man, Morgan. And I've been away for a while."

She doesn't seem to be following my subtle excuses to get rid of her, and she follows me up the stairs to the front door. Still uninvited, but I guess she's invited herself.

"Jack, this is me—Morgan." She says it like I could ever forget.

I let out an exasperated sigh, then sit her down with two hands to her shoulders. I need her undivided attention. She takes this to mean I want her here.

"I need to tell you something," I tell her, shrugging out of my jacket and throwing it against a chair. I start to roll up my sleeves, following her eyes as they trail up my arms.

"Before or after bed?" She smiles cheekily, and I realize I'm just going to have to rip this band aid off.

"I'm with someone," I tell her. It's a lie, but it's little and it's white, I tell myself.

She shakes her head as she looks at me in confusion, not entirely understanding what I'm saying.

"I'm with someone and it's serious. I'm going to marry her."

Morgan's face contorts as though I've just killed someone precious to her. She stands quickly, looks at me as though I've betrayed her, then slaps me. Hard. So hard, I can almost hear my ears ring. Okay, maybe I deserved that for lying, but not for wanting to be with someone else. She and I had been casual at best. No promises were made. No agreements. It was two old friends hooking up sometimes. So I'm not quite sure I understand why she's fixated on me, and to be honest, I don't quite care. All I know is I don't want her in my life when Olivia finds her way back to me.

CHAPTER 30

JACK

I am exiting the building just as a strong wind picks up and threatens to send lamp-posts and fire hydrants flying through it's tsunamic energy. I stop to raise the collar of my jacket and almost collide into a woman who seems to be in a hurry to enter the building I've just left. I sidestep to allow her access and come face to face with Olivia, her hair huddled beneath a beanie. I would have missed her altogether had it not been for the charge of electricity that surged through the air between us.

"Jack," she gasps, surprised to see me.

"Olivia," I acknowledge, nodding my head curtly. "You're a fair distance away from your side of town."

"I wasn't aware we'd drawn up lines so we wouldn't encroach upon one another's side of town," she laughs, removing her gloves and beanie. "I have a meeting with one of the curators here. I didn't know you were back in New York."

"Not for the duration. Just got in. Back to Cali in a week."

She nods her understanding and gives me a tight smile.

"You up for a coffee?" I ask her.

"I have my meeting."

"I'll wait if you have the time."

"I'd like that."

"There's a little coffee shop around the corner. Mario's. I'll be waiting there when you're done."

I watch her walk away, then smile when she turns back to look at me before disappearing into an anterior office. I walk to Mario's and order myself a coffee that grows cold while I wait at a window table in the back of the café. I'm glad the cafe's almost empty so I can have some much needed quiet time before Olivia walks in.

I think of her now, think how amazing it is that in a city as big as New York, I would run into her of all people. True, I had been contemplating calling her upon my arrival, but had not yet mustered up the courage to do so. There was only so much rejection that even I would take. Instead, by some amazing stroke of fate, I collide into her the same way she collided into my life a year ago. I've thought of nothing but Olivia in all the time I've been away. I'd heard the eventual news—of the wedding that never was, but in my head, I insisted I wasn't going to ask her about the break-up. I had honored her request to stay out of her life, therefore I couldn't have been the cause of the break-up. And even after the break-up, I'd kept my distance and remained low key, knowing full well that if she wanted me in her life, she would find me.

But Olivia had never called. In all the time she'd been single after breaking off her engagement, she had not called me. There had to be a reason why. I could think of only two possible reasons why she had not called me. Either she wasn't interested, (not likely, I thought—the charge of electricity that coursed between us every time we met was deathly), or there was someone else. It had to be one or the other. I could have kicked himself for not realizing it earlier. Of course, she agreed to coffee, I reminded myself. Who wouldn't agree to coffee with an old "almost friend" that they just ran into in the midst of a mini typhoon? Back and forth, I almost drive myself crazy with all the scenarios running through my head. My brain is so hung up on the fact that Olivia is probably with someone else that I almost get up to leave. Almost. But as I start to rise and leave, she stumbles into the coffee shop and races over to my table, hugging me close, then holding me at arms-length as she stares at me.

"Sorry, Jack. I forgot my manners back at the gallery. That was no way to greet an old friend. I was just surprised to see you, I guess."

I'm stunned as I fall back into my seat and she takes the chair opposite me, giving me a shit-eating grin. The waitress comes up by our table and takes our order, lingering a little longer than is completely necessary by my side.

"That waitress all but ignored me," Olivia points out.

"And you're upset, why?"

"Not upset. Just saying." She shrugs and slings her coat over the back of her chair.

"How did your meeting go?" I ask.

Olivia nods her head back and forth in a so-so motion.

I let out a chuckle and look at her beaming face. Her skin is pale from the cold, and her long, light brown hair frames her face in soft wide curls.

"I've missed you," I tell her, looking at her wistfully.

"You never called," she accuses me.

"You asked me to stay away," I shoot back, moving forward in my seat.

"Anything else I can get you?" the waitress asks, setting our coffees down before us, lingering yet again a second too long at my side.

Olivia looks up at the waitress incredulously, and a surge of rage, unwarranted at best, overcomes her suddenly. "Excuse me," she remarks dryly, "can't you see he's with someone?!?"

The waitress looks at her and smirks. Obviously, she isn't expecting her job to last long. "Sorry lady, but I don't see a ring on your finger," she snipes back, giving me a wink before she struts away.

"Un-fucken-believable!" Olivia fumes.

She looks over at me, watching me laugh hilariously, about to fall off my chair. I see the look on Olivia's face and straighten my back, a vain attempt at being serious.

"What was that?" I ask, laughter threatening to creep back into my voice again.

"Did you see that? What do two people have to do to have a decent conversation without the waitress slobbering all over the table?"

"I've never seen aggressive Olivia," I quip, my resolve breaking as I erupt into yet more laughter.

"Come on, let's go find another cafe," she says, rising from her chair.

◆ ◆ ◆

"So…. how's California?" Olivia asks, as we stroll down the street side by side, clutching our take-away coffees.

"Busy. Very busy," I tell her, a smile in my eyes.

"And you're going back in a week, you said?"

"Give or take a day."

"You never told me exactly what you're doing there, though." She frowns and looks at me questioningly.

"Does it matter, Olivia?" I stop walking and turn to face her. Olivia halts mid-stride and waits. "What does it matter what I'm doing there, Olivia? You never asked. You didn't want to know. All I knew was that you wanted to keep me at arm's length, and so I made it easy for you and left."

"But in the course of a conversation we're having, I can't ask what you're doing in California? Maybe because I'd be interested to know?"

She starts walking again and I follow suit.

"If I recall correctly, Olivia, the last time we spoke, you referred to me as a complication. So, this complication picked himself up and went to the opposite side of the country to uncomplicate things for you. I'm glad to see things have worked out for you, but that doesn't entitle you to ask questions you didn't want to ask when I was a *complication*."

She's silent momentarily while she digests everything I've said. I was right, of course—she had, in no uncertain terms, asked me to keep out of her life and had not so much as given me a backward glance. How could she now justify asking me personal questions she had no right to ask me?

"So, how about dinner tonight?" she asks.

THOMAS

Thomas's brain is ticking like a time bomb. He has been spending too much time overthinking, and now the strain is taking its toll. He wishes so desperately that he could retrace his steps... go back and do things over. He had not tried hard enough to hold on to Olivia. He knew this with a certainty, the same way he knew that Olivia had loved him at one point in her life. If only he hadn't screwed up...

"It's Jack," he whispers to himself. "It's always been Jack. Ever since she laid eyes on that wretched man, she hasn't been the same."

Max ushers Thomas into his office and tells him he's only agreed to see him as a courtesy for the role he had once played in his daughter's life.

"I appreciate you taking the time out of your busy schedule to meet with me," *Thomas manages, wincing at Max's slight. It hurt to constantly be reminded that he was no longer a part of Olivia's life, and he'd never be a part of the Kane empire, but he thought Max had a rude way of hitting him with the reminder.*

"An unfortunate turn of events," *Thomas agrees, crossing his right leg over his left as he takes a seat.* "I hope this does not exclude us from having mutual interests in the future."

Max looks at Thomas with some curiosity but says nothing. There is so much he could say—so much he wanted to say, but he kept his thoughts to himself as he wondered why Thomas was in his office.

"I want you to know, Max—my feelings for Olivia have not diminished in the least. If anything, they're stronger than ever, regardless of the outcome. And I *intend to spend the rest of my life trying to make her see that we were made for each other."*

Thomas watches as Max's eyebrows shoot up in disbelief. Although his formerly proposed father-in-law doesn't say anything, Thomas can feel the older man's disapproval invading the room.

"I thought the two of you had moved on," Max points out. "I know my daughter has."

"Regardless... I love Olivia and I want her back," Thomas says, and Max scoffs, incredulous. "I know it may seem hopeless, but I truly believe that the two of us can go back a few steps to a time when we were happier. And to do this, I am willing to do anything.... anything to regain her trust."

"So you're here to advise me of your intentions, then?" Max asks.

"I'm here to show you that I'm the best man for your daughter—and to ask that you aid me in putting a stop to this ridiculous charade between Olivia and Jack Speed. He is not a man you want on your team, nor will he be the son-in-law you require in your camp."

Max regards Thomas with fresh eyes. Finally, he understands. Thomas is here to ask for his help in booting Jack out of Olivia's life. However, as far as he knew, there was nothing going on between Jack and Olivia. In fact, he was certain that their friendship had remained.... just that, and that they hadn't seen each other in months.

"I'm not exactly sure I understand what your

concerns are, Thomas. Since you are no longer a part of my daughter's life, you are both free to associate with whomever you wish. Your concerns—though unfounded—are not exactly valid concerns when you are no longer engaged to my daughter."

"But I've already told you, Max, that status will change if I can have your word that you'll keep Jack at arm's length."

Max chuckles then pierces Thomas with a glare.

"I can't claim to know what the tipping point for you and my daughter was, Thomas—she refuses to talk about it. But what I do know for a fact is that you two are no longer together, and you therefore have no right to concern yourself with how she conducts her life. I will not interfere in my daughter's life, and she has made it abundantly clear that your engagement is off for good."

"He is the reason your daughter and I are no longer together. Jack came into her life and everything changed then—Olivia was never the same with me again."

"Whatever the reason Thomas, and I don't believe that to be the reason, what's done is done and you can't undo that."

"Then you leave me no choice..." Thomas says, reaching into his briefcase. He takes out a folder and slaps it onto Max's desk with a deliberate thud. Max looks at him but makes no move to retrieve the folder.

"Go ahead," Thomas nudges. "Take a look."

Max, although aware that Thomas is baiting him,

opens the file and scans the contents. A few sheets of paper, a couple of black and white photos, several newspaper clippings.

"I intend to get Olivia back," Thomas promises. "One way or another, with or without your help. Hopefully, there's enough incentive in that folder for you to help me reach my goal."

Max lowers the folder to the desk and regards Thomas with a piercing glare. "You hope to hold me to ransom with the contents in this file?" *he asks.*

"I'm merely trying to show you that I am the better man for your daughter. Put into perspective, you're a powerful man, running for a powerful government candidacy—how would a union between your daughter and an ex-con sit with your constituency? Especially after your last debacle with your suspected ties to the mob."

"So, in effect, you're hoping to blackmail me with Jack Speed's past."

Thomas shrugs nonchalantly. "If that's how you want to see it. It's not my intention, but if that's your interpretation, then so be it…." *he finishes.*

"Then let me make myself clear, Thomas. I am now starting to understand why my daughter left you. And under no circumstances, reasonable or not, will I make a deal with the devil. Now you take this file," *Max adds, throwing the file at Thomas,* "and you do with it what you will. I am under no compulsion to help you reunite with my daughter after your shameful show of disrespect here today."

Max rises from his seat and comes around his desk, looking down at Thomas square in the face. "And let me tell you another thing. Don't you ever, ever threaten me again. Should you see fit to tamper with my upcoming elections, you will bear the brunt of everything in my power raining down on you. I will ensure that you don't work a day in this city ever again. And that, my boy, is no threat—it's a promise." Max straightens himself without taking his eyes off Thomas, then quietly moves to the door, motioning without words that the meeting is over.

CHAPTER 31

OLIVIA

I hug my father as he walks into my office, his body enveloping me like a cocoon. He touches a finger to my nose as I pull away and offer him a seat.

"What will you drink?" I ask him.

My father waves me off and tells me he can't stay long. He regards me for a long minute but says nothing, and I realize this is not simply a visit to check up on me.

"What's going on with you?" he asks. "I haven't seen you in a while."

"It's been crazy busy since I've been back," I tell him, explaining my absence in his life. It has been hard settling back into work and life since my return.

"Well, it's great to have you back."

"I'm glad to be back, daddy."

"Anything special going on with you?"

I pause and give him a curious look; my father never pries, so I wonder what's on his mind.

He glances at me then down at the chaos that is my desk. I'm usually more organized, a neat multi-tasker who takes great pride in her work and the clean surfaces I need to carry out my day. He can see I'm not quite settled back into work, but he says nothing.

"So, Thomas is out of the picture," he starts finally. "How's Jack?"

I tilt my head to one side in query.

"It's funny you should ask that," I admit.

"Why's that?"

"We ran into each other a few days ago in Soho. I hadn't seen him in months, but there he was and we had coffee. But why would you ask about Jack specifically? What's on your mind?"

"I'm just curious."

"Dad, come on. This is me. Why would you ask about Jack?" And all of a sudden, I straighten and look at my father as alarm bells go off in my head. "Have you got someone following me?" I ask him.

"Son of a bitch!" my father mutters, almost under his breath.

"What's wrong?"

Dad takes a deep breath and sighs, looking at me.

"Thomas came to see me," he begins, sighing in resignation. "He's under the impression that he can win you back."

I scoff and shake my head in disbelief. "He told you about me and Jack? Is he following me?"

"Well, he must be if he knows you two met. The timing is too much of a coincidence, otherwise.

He seems to think that Jack is the reason you two broke up, and if Jack just stays out of the way, he has another chance with you."

"And your response?"

"I told him to leave the past where it belongs and move on. Obviously, the man has other plans."

"Other plans? What other plans? Jack had nothing to do with our break-up, dad. If anything, I hadn't seen Jack in months when I ran into him, and Thomas and I broke up more than four months ago, and I've been travelling, so I don't know what he's harping on about."

"This changes everything," Max says, calm but thoughtful. "Obviously, the man's going to extreme steps to remain in your life. He seems a little desperate to me. And I should tell you while we're at it, he had a dossier on Jack."

I can feel a fire slowly moving up my body to my face as it turns to stone. I have never told my father the full story of why Thomas and I broke up. I knew, with everything in me, that if Max knew what Thomas had done, he would kill him with his own hands, so I had spared him that. In sparing my father, I had also spared Thomas, who now seemed intent on insinuating himself in my life. The thought of him—just the mere mention of him, did things to my insides that I could not explain. I would have liked nothing more than to have him annihilated off the face of the planet, but not at the expense of my father, the man I loved and cherished most in the world.

Til now, I still bore the scars of Thomas's betrayal. My absolute rage at ever having loved him had turned to repulsion, and not just repulsion of the man I almost married, but also hatred of myself. After Thomas, I had run away. I had left everything that meant something to me and flown to the other side of the world to a retreat that would help me heal. I had been alone. And afraid. And resentful. His betrayal and hurt would mark me for weeks, months, maybe even years to come.

"What about Jack?" I snap out of my reverie, my voice almost a whisper. Jack's only just come back into my life. Naturally. As though the world has other plans for us, it refuses to keep us apart. I couldn't think past seeing him recently, and wanting to see him again. He was all I thought about. And I didn't want Thomas anywhere near that happiness I could see myself sharing with Jack.

"He's done some snooping into his past—tried to use that to blackmail me into keeping Jack away from you so he could move back into your life."

I gasp. Never ever in a million years would I have thought Thomas capable of such a thing. But then, I'd never thought him capable of those other things, either... But for him to think that he could worm his way back into my life? I would rather put him six feet under.

"What did he find?"

"I think that's a conversation you should have with Jack. If you're serious about this man, or you see him in your future, then you'd be interested to know. Otherwise, let sleeping dogs lie, Olivia. No good will come of asking about someone's past unless they want you to know."

"You said Thomas tried to blackmail you with the dossier?"

"He tried," Max admits, standing to his full height in preparation for his exit. "But I'm not going to let Thomas intimidate me into dictating your life for you. You know what's right from wrong. I trust you'll make the right decisions."

CHAPTER 32

JACK

When Olivia calls, I go running. I've lived my life in limbo for the past few months waiting for her to come back into my life. Truth be told, I haven't set foot in New York since the last time I left when she had dropped off the face of the earth and I had lost contact with her. Just knowing she was back in the city and that we were breathing the same air was enough to get me on the jet and heading back to New York to oversee matters I'd been sending others to deal with. Even the slightest possibility of running into her was enticing enough to bring me back.

But I couldn't have timed her return to my life any better. And I would never admit it, but my guy on the ground, Luke Mitchell's guy actually, has done a good job of getting his hands on her schedule and planting me directly in her path at the most opportune time. I feel like a stalker, but I'm determined to claim her heart before anyone else does and douse this fire she's lit within me. One day, she'll probably thank me for it. So it wasn't merely a chance meeting when we ran into each other at the Wyndham building; it was a carefully orchestrated accident that worked to my advantage. And Olivia's, I would say, as she seems happy enough to see me that she even suggested dinner.

She won't let me pick her up from her home, and I'm understanding of that. She wants her space and her privacy, and is not comfortable enough giving out her address after she relocated post her break up with Thomas. All this from Luke Mitchell—when the guy digs, he's meaner than an excavator. And even though I do have her address, I would never think to use it unsolicited. No. When I approach her home, it's going to be because she's invited me into her life of her own free will. It will be because she trusts me enough with her most personal information and wants me around. It will be what she wants to do, not what I want her to do.

We meet at Scallion by the Sea, a beautiful Italian restaurant on the water, and of course in my eagerness, I arrive with a few minutes to spare, and she rushes in shortly after, apologizing profusely for being late. I know she's not usually tardy; she's a punctual woman who sticks to a rigid schedule she doesn't waver from under any circumstances. I rise to greet her, and I can't help but wind an arm around her waist and pull her to me with a sense of familiarity as my lips touch the top of her head. I want this dinner to be as innocent as possible to put her at ease, so I don't kiss her cheeks or her lips, but I can't help wanting to touch her. So my hands around her waist it is. The lesser of two evils.

"I'm glad you called," I tell her as we sit down.

"I wanted to make the most of you before you flew away again."

She smiles, and the way her lips curl up into her dimples shatters me. She is sexy and beautiful and all the things I never knew I needed.

"There's one person that will keep me coming back to New York time and time again, Olivia," I tell her. She catches her breath in surprise. The implication of what I'm saying is not lost on her. I need to be upfront about my intentions towards her, and I need it to be known that she is the reason I will keep coming back to this city. I don't have a timeline of our relationship. I don't know in which order things will go, or how they will pan out, but what I do know is that I have my sights on her and I'll do anything to have her before anyone else steps in. I don't know how she feels about that, or how she'll feel about it once she knows, but all indications so far are that she's on board.

I'm holding her gaze when the waiter arrives to take our order. Olivia can't decide and I can't even look at the menu, so I ask him to bring out a selection of appetizers, then follow with a variety of seafood.

"You know he's going to bring out so much food we're not even going to eat." She laughs as the waiter hurries away.

Her laugh is infectious. I wonder how I've functioned without her the past few months, which have felt more like years. I realize how thoughts of her have softened me. Olivia is getting the best of me. I've been a bastard all my life, and now I'm a tame lion whenever I'm around her. She's smoothed out my edges, complemented my sharp lines with her softness, making me hunger for the sort of normalcy I've never craved before.

"So tell me what you've been doing since we last met," I enquire. I already know all the answers, but I want to hear it from her. I know what Luke Mitchell's guy saw, but I don't know what she felt or what she was thinking while she was away. Why she went away. I want to know the mechanics of her healing and why she felt she had to travel thousands of miles in order to heal from her ex.

She takes a deep shaky breath, as though it takes her much effort to talk about what she's about to say.

"After I broke up with Thomas, I felt like I had to get away, so I packed a bag and went to Bali."

"So far away," I murmur, my eyes never leaving her. "Why so far away?"

"No one knows me there. I went off the

grid, shutting down completely so I wouldn't be subjected to social media after the public found out we'd broken up. I knew Bali would be the best place to lay low and do some spiritual cleansing."

"And was it?"

She nods and tells me it was the best decision she made for herself.

"I think it was just what I needed when I needed it."

"Sometimes we don't know what we need until we're in the moment."

"Exactly. It was a good chance for me to do some soul searching. I nurtured my soul daily. Concentrated on myself and my own needs. Not what anybody else needed or wanted."

"Which, as I understand it, was exactly what you were doing before you left."

She looks at me like I've hit the nail on the head. "That's exactly what I was doing; giving everyone what they wanted while my own needs went unnoticed."

CHAPTER 33

OLIVIA

When Jack grabs my hand and pulls me toward the dance floor, I don't have time to argue with him. I don't even want to argue with him. I've never been much of a dancer, but I find I'm enjoying everything I'm doing with Jack. He puts a firm hand to the small of my back and holds me close as he moves me around the dance floor to the soft strains of Etta James. I can feel his breath on my hair like a soft blanket enveloping me as he tucks me under his chin and leads me around the floor. His scent is assaulting my senses; it's weaving its way into my bloodstream, coursing through my veins, ensuring I can never smell that scent again without remembering Jack. His scent is woodsy, spicy like the earth has met the sun mid-way. He holds me close, but it's not close enough. I want to be so close that my soul and his are touching in secret conversation. I want us to merge as one, and it's a feeling I've never felt before.

"So, tell me, Olivia, why it's taken us this long to wind up in this place." I swallow. Hard. I know exactly what he's asking. I can't see his face, but I know from the deep husk of his voice that he's been waiting patiently, and now he wants answers. We've been unresolved for so long. "If we hadn't run into each other the other day, would you ever have called me?"

The music stops and I draw away from him. He holds me at arm's length, unwilling to let me go any farther, and he waits for my answer. When I don't give him one, he leads me back to the table and holds my chair out for me. His proximity is shredding the last pieces of my sanity; he's too overwhelming. His scent, his voice, the feel of his hands against my skin. Everything about him is destroying me.

When he pushes my chair in, he doesn't make a move to his own chair. Instead, he leans in close to my ear so his breath is tantalizing my skin, and caresses me softly with his words.

"Once you're mine, I'm going to make you pay for every second you deprived me of being with you."

His words send a delicious shiver of excitement down my spine. He straightens and walks to his chair, unbuttoning his jacket before he sits as though nothing's happened. As though he didn't just send flames surging up my body. As if he didn't just threaten me with the tantalizing promise of what's to come. I squeeze my legs together, a warm sensation burning every aching crevice I have, and he fixes me with a knowing look. He's just as turned on as I am. Never in a million years would I have thought it possible to feel so much so quickly after the bad break up I've been through. But if I'm to fall, there's no one else I'd rather do it with than Jack Speed.

◆ ◆ ◆

We're half way through our dessert when the waiter approaches our table and advises me I have a phone call. I look at him like he's just flown in from outer space as he indicates the phone in his hand. It's cordless and I look at it in confusion before raising it to my ear.

There is no reply when I answer the call, even after repeated attempts to elicit a reply. There is only the heavy breathing of what I assume to be a male on the other end. I put the phone down and Jack motions the waiter over to collect it. Jack is watching me carefully, and I know I must look shaken, because he asks me who was on the line. His concern for me shifts my attention from the fear of a stranger breathing down the phone at me to the comfort of his presence.

"Are you still getting prank calls after all this time?" he asks, and I know he's thinking about that time in Sag Harbor when the same thing happened. Only this time, the caller hasn't dialed my own personal number, but the restaurant I'm sitting in, which could only mean one thing. Jack comes to the same realization at the same time I do, and slowly but surely, he skirts his eyes across the restaurant and to the windows beyond in search of the caller. After he signals the waiter for the check, he rises from his chair and extends his hand to me. I am stunned as I rise, the events spiraling too quickly for me to register. Jack has his phone to his ear as he leads me toward the kitchen and says something to the head chef about an exit. My thoughts are jumbled and incoherent as I follow him, my hand safely attached to his. No sooner has he barked orders down the phone, but he's dialing another number, and I'm in awe as I watch him manage the phone with one hand.

We push through a huge fire exit and emerge into an alley, where Jack looks up and leads me to a waiting car. I realize I've left my jacket behind but I don't even stop for it as I scramble into the car before it starts moving. Jack is still talking on the phone, something about security and a report, and probability. His voice is peppered with undertones of danger, and I can see by the way his eyes darken that he is furious.

"How often do you get these calls?" he asks, pocketing his phone.

"Not often. Not for a while now."

"Any idea who it is?"

I'd like to tell him that the answer is as

simple as a coincidence, but I refrain. The calls stopped while I was in Bali—but that could've been because I'd switched my phone off and wasn't dealing with the real world. I want to say they've become an unfamiliar companion, especially since I changed my number a while ago. But I don't. I try to wade through the jumble of my mind to figure out the last time I received such a call. It was in the time between my return from Bali and when I'd changed my number. I hadn't received any calls since then, which indicated the caller wasn't in my inner circle. And I had definitely been followed here tonight.

When I don't answer, Jack says my name, probing me for an answer.

"Whoever it is followed you to the restaurant tonight," he tells me, and I know he's just trying to bring home the danger in that fact. This could be a stalker. But it's too coincidental with the timing of Thomas's re-emergence for it to be that. It could only be him, especially after everything my father told me about their meeting. Thomas was hellbent on trying to get me back, and there was no telling what he would do in order to get there. Our last interaction had taught me that he is both unpredictable and unhinged. And a man who had nothing to lose was capable of anything.

CHAPTER 34

JACK

I can't say that I don't know what to do. I know exactly what to do. And I know exactly what I'll do once I find out who's stalking Olivia. We drive around the city in silence for a while, my hands on my knees itching to move toward her. I don't trust myself with her, so I sit in this position hoping to stem the desire that infiltrates my bones.

"We're clear," Willis calls, from the driver's seat. I've asked him to keep an eye out for any tails, and the good news is that whoever stalked Olivia to the restaurant is gone. The bad news is that whoever it is probably knows where she lives and where she works. Which means we've only lost him for the short haul.

"Can you take me home, please?" Olivia asks. Her voice is soft and broken, and she has gone off somewhere in her head and now she won't come back.

"Where were you before you met me at the restaurant?" I ask her. She gives me an odd look, weighing up my question. I think she understands what I'm getting at.

"At home."

"Which means that's probably where you were followed from. It's not safe for you to go back there."

"It's my home. I can't not go back there."

I don't know her well enough to know how far I can take this, but I need to take charge. She's not thinking straight and I can't let her go back home when there's an unknown element in the mix. I don't want to be faced with 'what ifs' if something happens to her. Not on my watch.

"I'll get you a room in my hotel. You'll be safer there."

Olivia starts to argue but I fix her with a glare that tells her she won't be getting her way this time. She moves back in her seat and bites her lip. I have no way of knowing what she's thinking, but I can see that she's worried, probably in more ways than one.

"Do you want me to call your father?" I ask, and she shakes her head vehemently. She is firm on keeping this from him, and I wonder what else she's hiding from him. And I wonder what she's hiding from me. Her face tells me there's something she's not sharing, something that I know I'm going to have to work hard to uncover.

◆ ◆ ◆

We're fortunate enough to get interconnecting rooms. When Olivia looks at me like I've lost my mind, I tell her under no circumstances am I letting her out of my sight until I can ensure her safety.

"But right next door to you?" she argues.

"Is where you'll be safest," I remind her. "You can go to your room when you want to sleep. I'll even let you lock the door." I give her a cheeky grin and she huffs past me as she passes through the interconnecting door to her own room with one of my shirts.

"When did you say you'll be going back to California?" she calls through the open doorway. I smile to myself. I know that right about now, she's viewing me as nothing more than a thorn in her side and is looking forward to the moment she gets rid of me.

"Actually, I've extended my stay," I tell her. There is complete silence as this sinks in. It's not what she's expecting. It's not even what I'm expecting. I haven't actually extended my stay, but now that I have her here with me, and we seem to be making headway, there's no way I'm leaving her. Especially not when there's a loose cannon out there somewhere.

A moment later there is a flurry of rustling and Olivia comes running into the room wearing nothing but my oversized shirt. She's drowning in it but I go almost crazy over her long tanned legs and bare feet. She plants her hands on her hips and fixes me with a bland look.

"And why are you extending?" she asks. She's irritated, and I know it's because she doesn't want me staying and bossing her around. I'm going to be doing a lot more than bossing once I have her over my knees.

"Business," I lie. "Some things have come up."

"Well, why don't you just make yourself a permanent office here, then!" And she throws her hands up in the air in an exasperated manner.

I admit that I've been thinking about doing that and I tell her so. She rolls her eyes in response and throws herself through the connecting door again, going into her own room, where she throws herself on the couch. She looks adorably sexy in my shirt, and I fight to tamp down my feelings as I watch her from the doorway.

"Olivia."

It's one word. It's me saying her name, caressing every vowel as it rolls off my tongue and into the room between us. She turns to face me. She's not really angry or irritated or any of those things she's pretending to be. She's just confused and afraid. Of her stalker. Of who it might be and the dangers to her. And maybe even a little afraid of me too. Afraid of what may happen between us. She may have wanted this at some stage months ago, but now she's in a different place. She's a different woman. With a different perspective than the one she had when I kissed her on her doorstep in the Hamptons. No less beautiful or enchanting, but she's still changed.

"Believe it or not, my main concern right now is your safety. I'm not going to leave you when there's a desperado on the loose who takes pleasure in breathing down a phone line at you."

"You can't save me, Jack. You have a life to live and your work is across the other side of the country."

"Why don't you let me decide where I choose to be?"

My phone rings. I ignore it for a moment, then reach into my pocket and answer, my eyes never leaving Olivia's. She watches me as I answer the call, and I can't help but think how damn beautiful she is. When I lower the phone, I run a hand through my thick wavy hair and let out a sigh.

"Why is Thomas Thackeray back in your life?" I ask her.

Three different emotions flicker across Olivia's face, morphing from one to the other as she considers my question. Shock. Then horror. Until she finally settles on fear.

CHAPTER 35
OLIVIA

"Why would you do this?" I ask him. I gasp, hyperventilating as I consider all the things that could go wrong in this scenario. Oh my God, I think I'm having a panic attack. I haven't had one in years, but the way my breathing is labored and my heart thumps out of my chest, I'm sure I'm having one.

"Olivia."

It's one word. He calms me with one word, and I forget that I can't breathe. I forget that I'm swollen with fear. I ignore all the old emotions flooding through me as I stare at him. He places two strong hands on my arms and steadies me with his gaze.

The place is swarming with... I don't even know what you'd call them. Guards. Mercenaries. Soldiers. I don't know what the hell he's done, but our hotel floor is surrounded with people who he explains are here to protect me. People who have been out in the hall all night, guarding and protecting. I know this because I ran into them when I opened my door in the early hours of the morning and found them there, preventing me from leaving. Jack argues with me that I'm not a prisoner, but under no circumstances will he let me leave the hotel and endanger myself.

And now my father is on his way to the hotel. I don't know how to explain any of this to him. And I wouldn't know how to start to explain why I'm here in this makeshift fortress with Jack Speed, surrounded by an army.

When my father does arrive, he views Jack with suspicious eyes. He takes one look at me then huddles me into his arms as he guides me to the couch. Jack tells him all about our dinner last night and the phone call I received at the restaurant. By the breath he exhales, I can see my father is grateful that Jack was with me when I got the phone call and was quick to take action.

My father fumes. He quietly simmers, then raises his eyes to meet Jack's, and a silent conversation takes place between them. I know that look—it's the look of two men with a plan, and it doesn't touch on anything legal.

"You can't possibly be mad at Jack for taking decisive action," he says.

"It's a little overkill, don't you think?"

"Not where your safety is concerned, princess." My father kisses my forehead and rises, putting a hand to Jack's shoulder in gratitude. "I have a friend in the NYPD," my father tells him. "I'll reach out, see what he can find out about

Thomas's whereabouts."

"You seem so sure it's Thomas." I rise quickly, facing my father, defiance lacing my voice. It's not that I want to protect Thomas, but what proof do we actually have that it's him?

"I know nothing if I don't know this," my father says, looking at me pointedly. "His reappearance coincided nicely with your return home. And his visit to me wasn't merely by chance. The man is hung up on you in a way that's unhealthy, Olivia."

I scoff and turn away from the men as shame lances through me. If only they knew. Thomas wasn't hung up on me. He was hung up on his tumble from the throne, and for a media whore like Thomas, that was far more dangerous than losing me.

"I don't think we have anything to worry about with Thomas," I tell them, looking from one man to the other.

"We have a lot to worry about," my father says. "I warned him off you and yet he still set his sights on you and followed you to the restaurant. As long as he's out there, you are not safe. You saw the way he attacked Teddy; the man is deranged."

"That's why we can't report this," Jack whispers, almost as though he's talking to himself. Something occurs to him, and he looks from me to my father, then back at me again. He never fails to undress me with just one look. "The police can't do anything until he physically hurts her."

I gasp. My father furrows his brows and studies Jack, silently requesting elaboration.

"They can't arrest him until he hurts her physically in some way. We can't wait for that to happen before they do something."

"That's why you've got a private army outside," my father surmises.

Jack nods once, slowly, a dark look passing between him and my father. An understanding. An agreement. They plan to do things their way, without the interference of the police. I don't know how far they'll go, but what I do know is that my father would do just about anything to protect me. Jack, I'm guessing, is of the same vein, and is not far behind my father in sharing the same view.

"I have men out looking for Thomas. And when they find him, he won't know what hit him."

◆ ◆ ◆

I feel compelled to tell Jack about Thomas's dossier. I don't know what's in it, but my father found it pertinent enough to mention it. I don't know how to raise the subject with him, but the opportunity presents itself once my father has left to attend to some business and we sit side by side on the sofa. Jack stretches both arms out against the backrest, taking a strand of my hair between his fingers as he looks at me with longing. He's too polite to do anything about it though, even though he may want to.

"I'm curious as to why Thomas found his way back to you now," he says, looking at me curiously.

"He came back because you did," I tell him, rubbing my palms together nervously as he looks to me for an explanation. "He mentioned you when he went to see my father a few days ago. I'm sure he was following me even then."

"What did he want?"

"For my father to help him scare you off and pave the way for me to take him back."

"And would you take him back?" he asks me. That he would even have the smallest doubt inside him shatters me.

"I knew what I was doing when I left him," I say. "There's no way I'll ever take him back."

CHAPTER 36

JACK

My phone is blowing up like crazy. I've managed to ignore it until now, but when Luke Mitchell calls me back to back multiple times, I know it's serious, and I walk toward the terrace, lifting the phone to my ear.

"Luke." My voice is anything but warm. I've switched to attack mode, and I need what he's got straight out without any beating around the bush.

"Jack, we've lost eyes on Thackeray," he tells me, his voice regretful. "He obviously knows someone has eyes on him."

This is not the news I want to hear. I work my jaw back and forth slowly, tamping down my anger. This was always a possibility, but the fact that it's happened has put me on my guard.

"Find him," I command. "And when you do, execute the plan as discussed. I'm not waiting on this."

I look through the glass partition at Olivia pacing around the room inside. She's getting agitated at the situation and the fact that she's had to put her life on hold. Again. I don't know how much longer I can keep her holed up here before she lets loose on me and demands that I let her leave. And she will do it, it's just a matter of time.

She stops pacing and looks up at me as I enter the room, a hopeful expression crossing her face. If only I could put her worries to sleep. But she doesn't know what she's up against with her ex, and if I'm to have any kind of a relationship with her, I need her present and I need her well.

"How much longer will I have to stay here?" she asks. She sees the light at the end of the tunnel. All I see is darkness.

"I'm going to shower then we can go out and discuss."

"Out?"

My eyes move from her face and slide down her body. Amy was kind enough to have some of Olivia's clothes sent over, and she's now wearing jeans and a shirt which hugs her in all the right places. She's sexy without trying, and I can't help the desire that floods my veins when I look at her. My hands move to the buttons on my shirt, starting at the top, and I hold her gaze as the shirt falls open, giving her an eyeful.

"We're going out," I tell her, the tone of my voice telling her there's no room for argument. "Be ready once I'm out of the shower."

I walk to my bathroom, shedding my clothes

the moment the door is closed. When I stand under the spray, I tip my head toward the wall, close my eyes and inhale a deep breath. It's all I can do to stop thinking about her. And all I can do to stop myself from reaching for my cock and yanking on it for some form of much needed release. I've been with the odd woman here and there in the past months—out of necessity—but now that Olivia is in my orbit, I don't want to be with anyone else, and I don't even want to touch myself. Even that I feel is like a betrayal to her. When I blow, I want it to be inside her.

The water is tepid at best, and when I feel like my body has had enough, I dry myself off and wrap a towel around my torso. I'm in my room getting dressed when I hear my phone ringing. I barely have time to zip up my pants and I'm walking through the house to the living room where I've left my jacket. I fish around in the pocket for my phone and go to stand by the window as I answer Selena's call. There's a problem on one of our construction sites downtown and she believes it's best I handle the situation myself.

"What's happened?" I ask her.

"It looks like someone has tampered with the wiring. Definitely vandalism. "

"Cameras?"

I insist on cameras at all our work sites, regardless of how fortified a construction zone we have. If the past has taught me anything, it's that cameras are a man's best friend when it comes to witness testimony. If there'd been working cameras when I ran into my spot of trouble when I was younger, so many things would have been different for me. It was for this reason that I insisted on regular maintenance and auditing of all cameras at any and all venues associated with GABLE. Our security and surveillance was second to none, primarily in a bid to prevent history repeating itself, the way I knew it so often had a tendency to do.

"Cameras stopped working," she says, and my heart drops when she tells me this. I know right then that this is definitely vandalism. Someone's fucking with me, because the cameras don't just stop working when someone is committing a crime. The idea that someone has tampered with my property rattles my ribcage and a dangerous fury comes over me.

"Pull every damn camera from every damn location within a three-mile radius. I don't care what you have to do. I want the footage in my hands in an hour."

I hang up with a heavy exhale and throw my phone at the window, where it goes scuttling to the floor in four different pieces as I mutter and curse and try to keep my rage under control.

"Ja…"

I turn my head at the sound of Olivia's

voice. Her gaze settles on my naked upper body, catching her by surprise, then moves to my phone on the ground, and back up again, resting on my back. I didn't have time to put on a shirt before I answered my phone, and I know under any other circumstances, she wouldn't have come running into my room but for the destruction she heard when I inflicted such pain on my phone.

Her eyes glaze over as she stares at my back, transfixed by the tattoo that stretches from one shoulder to the other and glides down almost every inch of my back. It's a massive soaring eagle, the fringes of its outstretched wings tapping my shoulders as its claws reach down for my lower back. I'm rarely if ever naked, so the existence of this tattoo is a tightly held secret shrouded in mystery. Not even the women I've been with could know about it unless they'd ever taken the time to put the light on while we fucked.

I decide to ignore Olivia's intrusion and pretend that nothing's happened. That's the best way to handle this without having to explain the tattoo or its origins. I know she won't ask; if I've learnt anything about Olivia, it's that she doesn't pry. And nor does she offer up any information without me asking.

"I'll be ready in two minutes," I tell her, ignoring the look on her face as she shifts her gaze to meet mine. I don't know what I see in her eyes, but there's no judgement there. Curiosity, maybe?

"I'm ready," she breathes, walking toward the sofa and taking a seat, effectively putting her back to me. I choose to ignore what happened where she chooses to give me the privacy I need. And for the first time in my life, I realize Olivia is the only woman I've ever come across who I don't need privacy from.

CHAPTER 37

OLIVIA

We arrive at a construction zone downtown where Jack points out his latest project, a multi-use residential building boasting fifty-four condominiums and a penthouse suite. He dons a hardhat and insists I wear one too before we make our way through the gate and meet the site foreman. It's a Sunday, so the site is deserted but for a few scattered personnel here and there who I assume have come in to deal with whatever disaster resulted in Jack throwing his phone at a wall. I realize the outcome of his anger is probably nothing new to Selena, who had a phone delivered to the front desk even before we left the building. Selena is nothing if not efficient.

"What do we have?" Jack asks, looking to the foreman as they bring up a surveillance feed.

"The cameras were definitely tampered with," he says, before another man steps forward and announces his presence, shaking Jack's hand. I gather he's part of Jack's security team, which has now extended its reach to all aspects of Jack's New York projects.

"What about the footage I asked for?"

"Right here," the man says, stepping forward and pressing on the keyboard. The screen lights up and a series of segments from different locations plays on the screen. "I think you'll be surprised with what you find," he tells Jack.

We continue to watch for countless minutes, and I recognize some of the more iconic buildings in some of the footage. It's mesmerizing watching how life on the streets of New York unfolds without anyone really realizing that at any given moment, their movements are being recorded or analyzed by strangers.

"There," the security guy points at the screen. And right before my eyes, there on the screen, is the undeniable proof that Thomas is walking less than 100 meters away from the construction zone at the time leading up to when the cameras went down. The shock catches in my throat as Jack slides his eyes quickly to me to gauge my reaction. I haven't seen my ex in months. I haven't seen him nor spoken with him, nor have our paths crossed. But the events of the past few days have been adding up to culminate in one agonizing realization; Thomas is back and he means to do serious damage to everyone around me in his bid to get to me.

The guard pulls up another set of camera angles that coincide directly with the time it would've taken Thomas to do the damage to the site and the cameras. In these slides, he's walking in reverse—away from the construction zone, and there's no refuting the evidence that is right before our eyes.

"Occam's razor," Jack whispers, so quietly I almost don't hear him. "We have to assume that Thackeray is the one responsible for this. And he's responsible for the calls to you."

"But to what end?" I ask, my eyes clouding in confusion. What could he possibly hope to gain from all this?

"In his mind, you destroyed him," Jack said. "For a social climber like he is, that's big. He's on a mission to destroy you the same way he believes you destroyed him."

◆ ◆ ◆

Jack takes me to an eatery by the water, and I suddenly understand his fondness for the sea. We sit at a table at the edge of the restaurant looking out at the water, a salty mist coating our skin. He's not taking any chances; he has security scattered at every entry and exit to the restaurant. There's security sitting indoors at two different tables watching us carefully, their hawkish eyes scanning the restaurant from time to time in their efforts to protect us. I don't know who this man is past a fleeting working relationship we had almost a year ago, and I don't think I want to know how he is able to summon a battalion of soldiers at such short notice to do his bidding. I don't care. All I know is that Thomas is back and that's cause for concern. I have seen first-hand what he is capable of and I never want to go back to that place where I am reduced to a pound of rubble underneath his feet.

"How did you leave things with Thackeray when you broke up?"

Jacks asks me this question but he has no idea what he's asking of me. The look on my face must tell him I'm horrified to be back there again, but he doesn't retract. Instead, his question gains more traction as his curiosity peaks. How can I tell him what I went through when I broke up with Thomas? How can I tell him I was attacked, almost raped had I not driven my key across his face, sending him howling to the floor in pain? How can I explain to him the trauma of what I endured without breaking down just remembering the terror of that day? And how could I ever protect my father from the knowledge of what I went through with Thomas?

"It wasn't pretty," I tell him.

When he realizes that's all I'm going to say, he cocks his head and shoots me an enquiring look, asking me to elaborate.

"Your interpretation of not pretty is probably different in comparison to mine," he says, his voice probing. "Are you sure there's not more to this than what you're telling me?"

"Would it make a difference?" I ask him. "You already know he's unhinged."

That wasn't the right thing to tell him, because I see the moment that a veil of black clouds shrouds his eyes, and it's like he's putting together the pieces of a puzzle. He knows I probably wouldn't outright lie, but I'd readily omit. My answer was just that—an omission. He seems to ponder my words too long, deciding against pushing any further, turning his attention instead to the calm lapping of the water.

"What are we going to do?" I ask him, my voice barely a whisper as I consider all the options before us. Maybe I should just leave and run back to Bali. Get as far away from here as I possibly can. That way I'm away from Thomas's reach and Jack can go back to living his event-free life without the burden of my problems.

Jack turns his face away from the water. He has one elbow leaning against the railing and he's clenching and unclenching his fist as his eyes glide over me.

"You're not going to do anything," he tells me. "You're going to go on with your life as you were and I'll take care of Thomas."

"What does that even mean?"

"It means I have a plan. One that will ensure your safety while we're trying to flush out

Thackeray. You're to stick to the plan at all times. I've run it past your father and he seems to agree it's the only way."

"I can't not go to work," I tell him. "I can't stay holed up in that hotel room—I'll go crazy."

"You won't have to. You'll be driven in to work. And you'll be driven home at the end of the day. You'll have security with you at all times until we find Thackeray."

"That's it? I can live with that," I say, shrugging.

"With one catch."

"Which is?"

"You'll have to relocate until we find him."

CHAPTER 38

JACK

I know she's hiding something the moment she deflects from my question and is reluctant to talk about her breakup with her ex. The same scumbag ex who's now wreaking havoc on our lives. He will not go quietly. And he will not simply fade into the background unless I make it so.

Once we're in the car leaving the restaurant, I tap Willis's shoulder and give him directions for an address on the other side of town. He knows the place well and gives me a short nod as he continues to drive. Olivia is staring out the window, avoiding me at all costs. She's too afraid to have a conversation with me in case I open up conversations which she doesn't want to have a bar of. I reach into my pocket for my phone and shoot off a quick message to Luke Mitchell. He may be all the way in California, but he could be anywhere in the world and I'd still get what I want from him.

Jack: Thomas Thackeray... I need his record unsealed.

Luke: That's a big ask.
Jack: Make it happen.

There's no response from Luke. I don't need one. It means he's already sprung into action and he's probably on his way to committing a crime or commissioning one. This is what I pay him for. And I pay him well.

When the car hooks a sharp left and glides into the basement of another high rise, Olivia blinks suddenly, as though coming out of a trance, and asks me where we are.

"Your new home," I tell her, getting out of the car. She sits looking at me, her stunned face telling me I probably should have given her a heads up. She didn't ague with me when I'd told her she had to move, but I think coming here was probably too much too soon and I should have prepared her better.

We stop at the bank of elevators, and I remove an access card from my coat pocket and swipe it into the reader before the elevator starts its ascent.

"Already?" she asks.

I let out an exasperated sigh. I don't think she understands how delicate a situation she's in. Putting off the crucial things could be the difference between a mistake and the sort of regret that only comes with hindsight.

"It's for your own good, Olivia. The sooner you understand that Thackeray will not let up until he's damaged you, the better off we'll all be."

"I can just leave the country," she says, her soft voice pleading. "I can go back to Bali—I made friends there and I was safe. He won't find me there."

My eyes darken as I look at her. She wants to run away. She wants to run. She'll be away from me. The thought of losing her again after finally finding my way back to her squeezes the life out of my heart. I'm not an easy man to break. But this would break me. Losing her, now that I've found her, would break me.

"You could do that," I tell her, not feeling anywhere near as confident as I sound, "but you would be running for the rest of your life. Men like Thomas Thackeray don't just simply disappear—he'll hunt you down forever if that's what he needs to do."

A shiver runs through her body, and she sways, my words knocking the wind out of her. I grab her arm, hold her upright as her body threatens to topple.

When the elevator stops, we step out and straight into an expansive living area, sparsely furnished, with windows looking out over the city. I stop and watch Olivia as she walks through the room, her eyes taking in her surroundings. She is spellbound.

"What is this place?" she asks.

"It's a place I purchased recently; it doesn't

make sense for me not to have a home here if I'm to go back and forth between here and California so often."

Her throat moves with unspoken words and she swallows her question whole as she continues to look around the room.

"It's so light. But where's all the furniture?" she asks, frowning when she suddenly notices what's missing.

"It's a work in progress," I tell her. "The previous owner left some things behind, but I haven't been here since I purchased it."

She approaches the sculptured concrete fireplace and presses her hand to the finish, gliding her fingers across the workmanship as she looks at it, awe-struck.

"What are your plans for it?" she asks. I swallow back the answer sitting on the tip of my tongue as a fire burns in the depths of my soul.

"I bought both apartments on this floor," I tell her. "The plan is to knock out the adjoining wall and create one big space."

I watch for her reaction carefully, waiting for her to ask the logical question that any other person would ask. Why would one person need so much space? But she doesn't say a thing; she just looks at me casually then looks away quickly as she tries to avoid the inevitable conversation that I'm hoping will unfold in its own time.

"You wouldn't be going to all that trouble

unless you were planning to spend more time here," she says, but to my ears, is sounds like she's asking a question.

"I wouldn't mind spending more time in New York."

I take a few slow steps towards her until we're standing barely two feet apart, facing one another. I've waited a year for her, and I will continue waiting as long as she needs me to, but something's got to give.

The look she gives me ignites the fire once again, sending a rush of heat through my body, from my toes to my head. It leaves me feeling punch drunk, out of sorts, and as though I'm having an out of body experience as I move closer to her until there is barely any air between us.

She's impossibly small in front of my hulking body, her petite frame fragile beneath my gaze. She looks at me helplessly, frozen in her spot as her head lifts to meet my eyes. She's the most beautiful creature I've ever seen, the most beautiful star in my orbit. And I can't believe she's finally found her way back to me.

CHAPTER 39

OLIVIA

There is a darkness in Jack's eyes when he stares at me. There is a storm brewing, matching my own, as he tells me he plans to spend more time in New York. He's telling me one thing, but I'm hearing another. His eyes talk to me in a way that his tongue never could.

I'm not immune to these feelings that are bouncing back and forth between us. I'd be foolish to deny them. More so after that kiss we shared in Sag Harbor when I had all but decided to leave Thomas. The kiss wasn't the thing that precipitated the break-up. It was the right thing at the wrong time, but that kiss… that kiss scorched my soul and left me wanting. That kiss had been everything. And it was everything now as we stood on opposing sides of a wall that neither of us was courageous enough to break down. We were so close yet so far. Barely inches apart, yet light years remained between us.

I had a fear, no matter how unreasonable it may have been, that if we didn't just jump in, we would miss our chance. And then the thought—

how many chances did a person actually get? We missed our chance months ago when I'd insisted on doing the right thing and breaking up with Thomas in person. That had ended in disaster and I had found myself on a plane bound for Bali. And now we had our chance, but neither of us wanted to overstep into the other's space. Into the great unknown. For a moment, I imagined my life a year from now. Then five years from now. Both times, I imagined Jack by my side, a mainstay and permanent fixture. If I were to go on and meet someone and live out the rest of my days with that someone, I didn't want that someone to be anyone but Jack.

His eyes are like blue ice as he looks down at me. His hair is matted back from his widow's peak. There are so many emotions swirling around in his eyes, and I read each one aloud in my head as I try to justify to myself the reasons I should take that leap of faith and just dive into the great unknown. He watches me with yearning, his eyes flicking between my own questioningly, wondering what I am thinking.

I'm barely a step away from him, and I take that one step forward, my chest nearly touching his. I'm afraid. So afraid, as I look at him and slowly build the courage needed to take the next step. And before I know it, Jack has taken a step into me and he's walking me backwards toward the wall, where he cages me in against the wall between two raised arms, fixes me with a penetrating stare and presses his lips against mine.

He's soft and warm and the feelings he evokes in me cause my heart to scatter; I could swear there's no blood pumping into it as I lose my balance and fall into him, losing myself to the moment as our tongues lash at each other in their own little happy dance. The kiss sends sparks and stars shooting before my eyes as I melt to his touch.

Our chemistry is off the charts, and we continue to move into each other like we can't get close enough.

Jack lowers his arms until his hands are resting on my hips, pulling me further into him, his hold on me both punishing and brutal. Punishing in a way that tells me he wants me and has waited for this moment for too long. Brutal in a way that tells me in no uncertain terms that I now belong to him.

I moan into his mouth, pressing my body into his. Boy, do I want him. More than anything. But I haven't been with a man in so long, and I think I've forgotten how to conduct myself. There's also the matter of the scars I carry after Thomas's attack. I try to push all thoughts of Thomas out of my head at the same time that my body stiffens and Jack feels the change in our chemistry. He pulls away and looks at me with a question in his eyes, wondering why I've suddenly shut down.

It's not something I can help; it's an automatic reaction I revert to any time Thomas crosses my mind. But instead of putting pressure on me to answer, he takes my hand and guides me through the rest of the apartment, pointing out each room as we access it.

I follow him shyly as he pulls me along, his hand never letting go of mine. Even when he stops and announces the room we're in, he doesn't let go. He won't let go. As though in doing so, he could lose the connection between us.

"What do you think?" he asks, looking at me expectantly after giving me the tour.

"That's a lot of space for one person," I comment. I'd told myself I wouldn't go down this road, but here I am.

"I don't want to move or renovate again if I outgrow this place," he tells me.

"Why did you bring me here, Jack?"

"You'll stay here until we deal with Thackeray," he tells me. He doesn't suggest it. He tells me. Commanding, controlling. On anyone else, it wouldn't fly. But on him, domineering is the new mood.

"Here?" I'm gob smacked. "With you?"

"We won't be spending every waking hour here, Olivia. We'll both be at work. This high security building is a safe place for you to come to after work. No one gets in or out unless they live here. No one."

"Where will you be?"

He sighs. He knew he'd have to put up this fight. "If it makes you feel better, I'll stay in the apartment next door. Although I don't see why we can't both stay here—there are two bedrooms, after all."

"I'm not sure this would be the proper thing to do," I stress. This was perhaps moving way too fast for my liking.

"Define 'proper'. Don't act like that kiss meant nothing, Olivia."

We've danced around one another every time we've found ourselves together in the same room. There's no denying the sizzling chemistry between us. It's as undeniable as it is potent. And I can't be the one that throws this thing between us out the door before it even gets started.

"That kiss meant everything I never knew I wanted."

CHAPTER 40

JACK

My heart is doing little cartwheels as I watch Olivia walking around the living room, her phone fixed to her ear as she talks to her best friend Amy. She looks beautiful as always, but she's resplendent in the sunlight that filters through the windows from the late afternoon sun.

My own phone chirps and I look down at it. It's Luke, asking me to call him when I can. Then he adds that he wants to speak to me when I'm alone. He knows I'm with Olivia—I've already briefed him and the extra security are all members of his own team whilst he works on recruiting some ex-Navy Seals to take on Olivia's security detail. I've never had a reason to insist on huge security measures, but now with Olivia in my life and Thackeray on the loose, I am pulling out all the stops. I will take the issue of her safety as seriously as I have to in order to ensure that her ex doesn't come in contact with her in any way, shape, or form.

"I would keep that girl of yours away from Thackeray no matter the cost," Luke says, as soon as he picks up. The fact that he refers to Olivia as my girl makes my heart sing. He doesn't know the mechanics of my relationship with her, but I guess he would've put two and two together considering all the effort I was going to for her.

"This can't be good."

"That's because it's not," he confirms. "I'm lucky to still have friends on the force."

"What did you find?"

"A thread that led me right to the officer that was in charge of the case that Thackeray was involved in. He knows exactly what's in those sealed records."

"Shoot me."

"Apparently while he was in college, there were a spate of rapes on campus that were attributed to one person."

My heart, which was most recently doing happy laps around the room now stops. My blood runs cold. And I am livid.

"Thomas Thackeray," I guess.

"The evidence, once confronted with it, was overwhelming. His parents paid a king's ransom to keep the victims out of the courts and the news out of the press. The records were sealed because someone owed the family a favor."

"How may rapes are we talking about?" I ask him.

"Four on campus. Two burglary/rapes with the same MO off campus—in neighboring areas, with both victims also picking out Thackeray in a line up."

"What are the chances?" I mutter to myself. "You're absolutely sure it's the same Thomas Thackeray?"

"How many Thomas William Thackeray the Thirds do you know?" he asks me, and I have to nod in agreement, as though he can see the action through the phone.

"It gets worse, Jack."

I brace myself. I know sometimes there are things I'm better off not knowing. I don't have a weak stomach, but I know what I'm capable of if someone hurts one of my own. Mercy is not necessarily a word in my vocabulary.

"What is it?"

I need to know exactly what Thomas Thackeray is capable of.

"His trip to Mexico. Two women who worked in the brothel where he stayed reported being attacked by him. One so severely, she eventually succumbed to her injuries and died."

Murder. The man has committed murder. There is a sharp intake of breath as I consider all the elements of what I know about this man. He is a monster, there's no two ways to spin this. And God only knows what he'd done to hurt Olivia. The way she clamped up suddenly earlier wasn't something that just happened. There was a trigger, and there was something she wasn't telling me. I had to get her out of her head. And I had to know what damage Thomas had done to her.

"Jack?"

Luke's voice brings me back to the present. I'm listening to him, but I can't hear a thing he says as my eyes follow Olivia around the room. I ask him to back up when he throws in the word bankruptcy, and he starts to repeat his words over.

"The man is steeped in massive debt. His parents lost almost everything cleaning up his college mess. They're on the verge of bankruptcy. In my opinion, that's why he sought out Olivia Kane."

My neck bristles and my body hums with anger. How could any man not possibly love a woman like Olivia? I knew that he was a social climber, but that he would prey on her simply for what she could do for him financially gives me pause for thought.

"What makes you say that?" I ask him.

"You have no idea the sort of financial trouble Thomas is in without the backing of the Kane name."

"What about his high paying job on Wall Street?"

"He lost it months ago. There were no notes on file, but there are indications of fraud."

"How bad is it?" I ask him. If the money train

he'd been riding on with his parents had dried up and he no longer had a job, his financial status was questionable.

"Bad enough that he's maxed out his credit cards so we can't track him through those."

The man is running on empty fumes. Olivia would have been his gateway to an immense fortune. Her leaving him has deprived him of that. Her leaving left him with nothing, reducing him to insignificance. This was no more apparent than the numbers Selena had rattled off to me when the news of their breakup was announced to the world via a statement released by Olivia's legal team. In the few short months that they were engaged, Thomas's social media following had steadily climbed from 154k to 7.5m, steadily increasing with every photo he posted of them together as a couple. As soon as they were over, the numbers had started dropping until they were less than half of what he had initially started out with. It was not hard to grasp who had been the more popular partner in that relationship.

I swing my eyes toward Olivia. She's finished her call and is now standing across the room watching me, a puzzled look on her face. I assume the look on my face as I digest what Luke's saying is what's caused the apprehension on her own.

This situation is so much worse than I could have anticipated. Olivia didn't just break off her engagement to that psycho. She basically annihilated him. I don't even think she understands the severity of what she's done. And I'm the first one to put my hand up and admit that the worst type of man is one who has absolutely nothing left to lose.

CHAPTER 41

OLIVIA

Jack is an extremely handsome man. I watch him move around the room with the practiced grace of a bull. He's built like a tank, all muscle and sinew and strength as he flows seamlessly from one call to another, conducting his business with the schooled precision of a man who knows exactly what he's doing. He's flung on a black t-shirt that doesn't show a peek of the tattoo that covers his body and low slung jeans which sag against his ass with just the right amount of fabric to make my mouth water.

My own wanton need surprises me. I have not been interested in another man in so long, and I don't recall a time—ever—that I've actually desired a man like this. Thomas, I had come to realize, was something I fell into because he was there. He had bumped into me in a coffee shop, where I spilt my coffee on him and had felt obliged to have a coffee with him when he asked because of the mishap. One coffee had turned into two and we'd gone from there. He'd been easy to talk to, charming. But hindsight was such a lovely thing when you could finally see again. Because I could now see that everything in my life after I met Thomas had been geared a certain way. Almost engineered. Orchestrated. The way he wanted things to be. And I, falling into my first serious relationship, had just gone along with everything he'd said or done. As though brainwashed.

When Jack looks at me now, it's with a certain trepidation. There are questions in his eyes, and I know instantly that not all his phone calls are business related. He wants to ask me things, maybe dissect my life a little, but he doesn't know how far he can push. And I don't blame him. We don't know each other well enough to understand which lines we can cross without repercussions. But we'll need to learn.

I decide to take the first step and give him a small smile. The kiss we shared earlier still tingles on my lips. I liked it and I want more of it. I want more of his hands on my hips, holding me to him. I want his hand in mine, a sign of his claim on me. And I want everything he has to offer and more. In good time.

"So I'm going in to the office tomorrow," I confirm.

He gives me a short nod and agrees, then tells me he'll drop me off in the morning, and security will stay in the building at the lift entry to our floor.

"You cannot leave the building unless you're with your security detail, Olivia."

"I really think this is a little overkill," I say, laughing him off.

Jack is deadly serious when he addresses me again. I've never seen this side of him, and I know he's not one to over-react. If this weren't serious, he wouldn't be portraying it as such.

"I need you to understand the sort of man we're dealing with here."

"I know the sort of man he is," I remind him. "I was with him for more than two years."

"You could have been with him a lifetime and still you wouldn't understand the sort of man Thomas Thackeray is," he says, and the way he says it causes goosebumps to dot the length of my arms.

"I don't think he'd try anything with this much security around," I insist.

"How did you two meet?" he asks me. "You never told me."

"You never asked. And why are we talking about him, anyway?"

I stand and throw my arms around casually, indicating Thomas is the last thing I want to discuss. I want to do everything in my power to rid myself of any thoughts of him and move on with my life.

"I understand your reluctance to talk about him, Olivia. I do."

His voice is soft and coaxing, the rich smooth syrup of his cadence forcing me to stare at him in wonder. Here is a man who needs to make no effort to get whatever he wants out of me.

"You need to remove him from your life completely before you can forget him and move on. That's not going to happen until we find him. Otherwise, he'll always be a danger to you, Olivia."

His words give me pause for thought. A ripple of fear makes its way up my spine and I feel the color draining out of me. I wonder if he knows what happened between Thomas and me that day? But how could he possibly know? But the way he's probing into my soul, his eyes asking me a silent question. He knows but he doesn't want to say it. He wants me to tell him. And I don't know that I can.

I feel my whole body tense, my hands clenching at my sides as I stare through him, lost in my thoughts. How would his knowing change what happens next between us? How will he see me when he knows what a weak person I was to go along with an engagement I didn't want? Then to put myself in a position where I'm almost raped. And to finish off, the fact that I just ran away without confronting my problems. Without dealing with them? He's the most logical thinking person I know; I don't see any logic in any of what I've done in regards to Thomas, and I don't know how that's going to affect him if he knows.

"Olivia?"

I shake my head until I snap out of my thoughts and focus my misty eyes back on him. The thought of losing him just when I've found him again is causing a deep sharp pain in my heart. He's crossed the room and his hands are at my hips again. His eyes are worried as they assess me for a few endless moments.

"What?" I ask him.

"What did he do to you?"

He finally asks the question, and that's when I realize he probably already knows. He knows something, because there's no way he could've just guessed.

"I don't want to talk about it."

I'm hyperventilating again as my heart beats out of my chest, and I'm afraid that if I don't catch it, I'll spiral into another panic attack.

"What did that fucking bastard. *Do. To. You.*"

He is so angry. His anger makes my body sway and I could swear the whole building rattles. He locks his jaw, and in my shock, I could swear that his eyes turn black. He's not angry, he's murderous. And the fact that he's murderous over me makes me want to throw my arms around his neck and kiss him silly. But I don't. This is serious. And I don't want to think about what he may do to Thomas if he ever catches up with him.

CHAPTER 42

JACK

We drive to work in silence. I make no move toward Olivia as she sits on the opposite end of the seat looking out the window. I watch her quietly; even with her face turned away from me, she is the most beautiful woman. The crane of her neck is doing things to me that destroys me for all other women.

Last night, I learnt a few things about myself. Actually, I finally understood a few things about myself and Olivia. Whatever Thomas did to her doesn't change a damn thing in my books, except that the animal will pay dearly once I catch up with him. I don't need to know the details; I will spare her the pain of recalling things she wants to forget about. But I will not forget that he hurt her, and I will make sure that he pays.

She's full of shame. It's not her fault, but she's overcome with a sense of shame over what's happened, and I don't know what to say to her to make things better. I'm out of my depth here, and I don't want there to be this void between us.

When I drop her off, I watch her walk into

the building with two security guards at her side. They're armed and they know to stay with her at all times. These are my explicit instructions, and they're paid well to do as I request. I've also got Amy and Ainsley on board with her protection; they'll keep a close eye on her and alert me to any issues that may arise. I know that Olivia wouldn't lie to me, but would she keep things from me to spare me what she deems to be unnecessary concern? She most definitely would.

I hate that we've left things this way. After our little chat yesterday, Olivia retreated to her own room which I'd pointed out to her earlier and hadn't come out again, not even to eat. She'd slept on her side of the apartment, and she'd woken and prepared herself for work without so much as a word past a greeting in passing.

Selena calls as the car pulls away from the curb. She knows literally everything that's been going on the past few days and she's been a godsend to both Olivia and myself, arranging for some of our personal effects to be sent over to the condo to ensure at the bare minimum a semi-comfortable stay for the next few days.

"I've re-organized your schedule to free you up at midday," she confirms, and again I'm grateful for the way she's able to work her magic and shift things around so I get what I need.

"Where are we with the Seals contract?" I ask her.

"Waiting on your signature."

This is why I will never let go of Selena. She's the most efficient PA I've ever had and she's worth every cent of what I pay her. And then some.

◆ ◆ ◆

Her door is open when I approach Olivia's office at midday. She has her head down in concentration, her eyebrows folded in as she studies a set of drawings. She is so invested in what she's doing that she doesn't notice me standing there watching her, admiring the sleek curve of her neck as she rubs a thoughtful hand against it. She is beauty and splendor and everything I never knew I wanted in a woman, and she leaves me breathless at every turn.

I stroll into her office casually, and for the first time she looks up in surprise and notices me. She's not expecting me and she watches me curiously as I approach her desk, my hands in my pockets as casually as though I've done this a hundred times before. She sits back in her chair and waits, tongue tied, and dare I say a little happy to see me.

"I thought we'd go out to lunch together," is the only thing I can offer her. Her eyes twinkle as she suppresses a shy smile and tells me she's swamped with work. "I know you're not too busy to eat."

It amazes me how easily Olivia gives in to me. She stands and places two firm hands on her desktop to steady herself, then grabs her bag and walks toward me. I grab her hand in mine and she looks down at the bridge I created between us. I don't know what she's thinking. Whether or not she thinks it's too soon. Or if this is the right way to announce that we're together to her colleagues. Or even just the fact of there being no label to what we share. All I know is she is now in my life and this is where I aim to keep her, label or not. I'm feeling things I can't even start to explain when it comes to her, and I want more of it. I want more of her.

"Are we doing this?" she asks, smiling down at our entwined hands.

"We're doing this."

We've taken one step toward the door when Amy comes bustling through the door with a sheath of papers in her hand, almost knocking us over in her haste. She stops short, spies our clasped hands, then raises her hands, palms up, as if to say she won't be the one to break up this party. I know she's happy for us; she's indicated as much when I've spoken with her on the phone, and she slides deftly to the side and bids us farewell in three different languages as we make our exit.

"There's a sushi place down the street," I tell her, as we stroll along the street, hand in hand.

"I know it. We're walking?" Again, I've surprised her.

"Don't worry," I murmur, pulling her into me. "There's security everywhere."

She's bound to me eternally when she literally pastes her body closer to mine, hip to hip, and weaves her hand around my waist. She rests her head against my arm like she was always meant to be there. And something deep inside me roars, a deep awakening coming to life as I understand what she's come to mean to me. I would do anything for this woman. And I will do everything in my power to make her mine and keep her safe.

CHAPTER 43
OLIVIA

I've crossed over that line where Jack was a bit player in my life, a sort of salvation, to where he's become everything. We have separate rooms in his condo in progress, but there may as well be no walls between us as we relegate ourselves to our independent corners but our thoughts lay firmly with one another.

I know I must mean something to him, for all the trouble he's going to in trying to keep me safe and comfortable. And I'm not going to deny what he means to me. The very thought of not having him in my life is no longer an option.

I look up when there's a knock at my door, pause then get up to open the door. Jack is standing there in sweats that ride low on his hips and a loose t-shirt that is drenched in sweat. There's a towel around his neck that he uses to wipe at his face.

"Your father is here."

I follow him out to the living room and greet my father, who stands anxiously waiting for me.

"I didn't know you'd be coming." My eyes sweep

over him anxiously, and he flicks his eyes from me to Jack, then back again.

"I'll give you guys some privacy," Jack says, excusing himself to shower.

My father folds me into his arms and kisses my forehead, the way he used to when I was a child. There is a tightness in his voice as we catch up on the past few days and what we've each missed of the other's life.

"What's wrong?" I ask him.

"Are you comfortable here?"

He looks around the room, takes in the lack of furniture, and gives me a confused look.

"Jack brought me here because of the level of security."

"It doesn't look lived in."

"It isn't usually. He's got plans to renovate before he moves in. Thomas doesn't know this place, so consider it safe."

My father bristles at the mention of Thomas. He holds me at arm's length and inhales shakily in a way that tells me there's something on his mind.

"Jack didn't think it a good idea for you to stay with me," my father explains. I make it known that I have to agree with Jack, and that's why I chose not to stay with any one of my family or friends where Thomas could so easily find me.

"I need you not to worry about me," I tell him, trying for reassuring, but knowing my skills of persuasion are falling flat.

"Of course I'm always going to worry about you. You're my daughter, my only child. It's my job to protect you."

"You needn't carry the burden on your own, daddy."

I smooth a hand up and down his arm, alarmed at his concern. I've never seen my father this way. When he shoots his eyes to the doorway, I regard him carefully. I look over my shoulder, but there's nothing to see, and I wonder once again about the nervous tension radiating off my father's body.

"What's really on your mind?" I ask him.

He shakes his head like it's nothing, then looks up at me with concern in his eyes. "That matter we spoke about a few days ago. The dossier."

My mind immediately flits back to my father mentioning that Thomas has a dossier on Jack. I don't understand why it's become of some significance now.

"What about it?"

"I don't know how safe you are with Jack."

My blood curdles as my father's words register in my brain. A couple of days ago, Jack and my father were in agreement over how best to address the issue of Thomas and deal with my safety. Now it seemed like my father had done an about face and was no longer convinced that Jack's presence in my life was such a good thing.

"Why do you say that?" I gasp.

"Because he's been digging into my past," Jack says, coming into the room in a fresh pair of sweats, his hair still wet from his shower. I turn where I stand, caught off guard, feeling like a guilty child. I feel like I'm wedged between a rock and a hard place as I look from one man to the other, trying to decipher the look passing between them.

My father straightens to his full height, looking like he's preparing to do battle, while Jack saunters easily into the room, pours drinks and hands them out before he takes a seat on the sofa. He leans forward and stares down into his glass, a thoughtful look crossing his face as he chooses his words.

"I don't advertise my past, but I won't ever lie to you about it if you want to know."

He addresses the room, but his eyes swing my way. They are so desolate as they ask for forgiveness. I know whatever it is, he never meant for me to find out this way, and he's afraid of the judgment he'll face when I find out.

"She has to know," my father prompts. I know he's just trying to protect me, but I don't know what wisdom will come of me knowing about Jack's past. I don't know what my father hopes to accomplish.

"I thought you said not to go digging into the past," I remind my father.

"That was before all this with Thomas. I don't

know who to trust when it comes to you, Olivia."

"You know you can trust me," Jack says, looking to me for confirmation.

"Just tell her," my father commands. "Either you do or I will."

Jack inhales a sigh of resignation and licks his lips, starting at the beginning.

He tells us about how he came from nothing and worked his butt off academically, winning a scholarship to Stanford. He describes in minute detail every little circumstance that led him to be at a celebratory dinner and how he came to be involved in a brawl that ended up with one guy dead and countless others injured. My mind races at a thousand miles an hour as his words sink in. And I'm terrified of what he'll tell me. If for no other reason than I wish I could spare him the pain of what he's been through.

"I tried to break up the fight. Isn't that what any upstanding citizen would do? But when I pulled the brawlers apart, I did it with such force that one of the men ended up falling and hitting his head on the pavement. He died and I spent two years in prison for involuntary manslaughter."

My hand flies to my mouth in stunned silence as I consider everything he's told me. My father was right; we should have left the past where it belonged. But now that I knew, there was no avoiding the knowledge he'd bestowed upon me.

CHAPTER 44

JACK

When Max leaves the apartment, satisfied that he's done what he needs to do to give his daughter all the facts as presented to him, I can't say I'm not a little resentful that he forced my hand in this way. He believes in doing what he's done, he's protecting his daughter. I believe now is not the time to put doubts in her head, not when her safety is at stake. Knowing something like this is epic and could drive her from the safety of my arms. And that's the last thing I want to happen.

"We good?" I ask, coming back into the living room after I've seen her father out.

She turns eyes full of sorrow in my direction. She's in pain and she's hurt and confused, and I don't know how to fix this. We're just getting started and now she has to deal with my criminal past. I don't know what she's thinking.

For the longest time, she doesn't say anything. I need to know what she's thinking, but instead she gives me her silence.

"Your past is your past," she says finally, and I can almost feel myself exhaling. "My father never should have cornered you like that."

"I understand why he did it," I tell her, sitting down beside her, leaving a comfortable distance between us.

"Regardless. That one piece of your past doesn't define who you are now. I mean, look how far you've come since then."

"It doesn't bother you that I've been to prison?" I ask her. She couldn't be more perfect for me.

"Not one bit. I can't believe this is the thing that Thomas threatened my father with."

"He threatened your father?"

"Indirectly. He told him if he didn't help him keep us apart and convince me to go back to him, he'd make your past public to destroy my father's run in the next election."

"I have no doubt he'd do it," I tell her. She probably doesn't want to hear it, but Thomas will stop at nothing to get what he wants.

"Will it hurt you if he does?" she asks, and I know she's referring to my business dealings. I shake my head. If anything, that's the last thing she needs to worry about. My conviction is public knowledge, and it's also well documented that what led to it was an unfortunate accident. I had no reservations when it came to my past; if anything, anyone seeking to invest in any of my companies would have done their research and would know my backstory. This is what smart businesspeople do. So for me to be concerned with people finding out about my past was invalid. The only person I was concerned about and whose opinion I valued was sitting right in front of me.

When Olivia places a hand on my knee, I feel the burn of her touch as it seeps through the fabric separating us. She gives me a demure smile, telling me everything's going to be okay, and it's just what I need to hear after the past hour of walking a tightrope as I relay my past to her. She now knows everything she needs to know about me, and I feel like the weight of her knowing has been lifted from my shoulders and placed squarely in a neat box between us.

"Does this now mean you'll tell me about your tattoo?" she asks, taking advantage of our hour of enlightenment.

"Maybe someday when you're ready to hear it," I tell her.

"You don't like to talk about it."

"I'd rather spend our time together talking about important things."

"Anything to do with you is important," she tells me, a blush rising up her neck as she bumps her shoulder into me.

I can't help but reach up and weave a hand around her neck, bringing her in to meet my lips. Her mouth is pillowy soft as we touch, and although we've started out slow, it's not long before I'm losing control of myself and my hand is messing through her hair, holding her in place. I don't want to come up for air and I don't want to let her go. All I want to do is live and breathe and die in her embrace. She moans into me and lifts her arms, folding them around my neck, pressing her chest into mine until she's almost climbing into my lap. I pull her to me and stand, lifting her legs until they're wrapped around my waist, my mouth still sealed to hers as I carry her to my bedroom.

"This is your last chance to tell me to stop," I murmur into her between kisses as I glide my lips across her face and down the length of her beautiful neck. "Tell me to stop," I breathe.

"Who says I want you to stop?"

Her words make me mad with desire, and I am feverish as my mouth lunges for her again. There is nothing and no one in this world I want right now more than Olivia. She's the unexpected gift I didn't know I'd been waiting for. The surprise that hit me unaware like a comet hurtling through space. And I can't get enough of her.

I breathe into her and she reciprocates. Closer, closer, I can't get close enough to her. I need us to be as one. One body, one mind, one soul.

One love.

She's doing things to my brain I can't explain. My thoughts are jumbled, my past and my present no longer in my vision. All I see now is my future. A future with Olivia. Everything else now sits firmly in my rear-view mirror; of little or no importance unless she calls on it and wants it to be. She's my future and my life, the one all-consuming certainty that I know will always be there.

I lay her down on the bed, take a step back and admire her body as it lays where it's meant to. This is the moment I've waited for. And this is the moment from which there'll be no coming back. Once I make her mine tonight, that cannot be undone. Because once Olivia Kane is mine, she's mine eternally.

CHAPTER 45

OLIVIA

Everything seems to fall into place as I get to work on several projects that Ainsley throws my way. She's taking baby steps, but I'm literally begging her for more. Anything that will keep me busy and keep my mind off the security measures that have been put into place to dog me no matter where I go. I don't know how people actually handle this sort of thing, or how they can manage strict rules about where they can and can't go. Although I'm introverted by nature, mentally knowing that I can't go somewhere does take somewhat of a toll.

I spend the afternoon following up on sketches and returning some missed calls. These days, I'm most happiest in those last few hours before the day is over and I can head home and catch up with Jack. There's a certain sense of urgency to our relationship now that we've gotten to know each other better, and I can't help but wonder at the amazing man that he is.

When 2pm rolls around, all hell breaks loose at work. The fire alarms in the building go off, and I listen to the frantic rush of employees as they scuttle past my office toward the fire exits. Amy ducks her head in and tells me to get my ass moving and I nod, telling her I'm on my way, before she marshals the rest of our staff through the hallway. I shuffle some papers on my desk and square them away, getting ready to leave.

A fire emergency is the one thing we haven't anticipated, and therefore the one thing our security team is not trained for. As people rush to file out of the building, I can only imagine what my security is thinking as they're prevented from entering the building. The one absolute in a fire evacuation is that no one enters the building until the fire brigade arrive. It's a rule that everybody takes seriously, not least of all building security. I know my security team will be running around like crazy trying to find me in the melee of exiting employees, so I don't want to keep them waiting.

Knowing that no one is allowed into the building is how I know no one's coming back for me. It's also how I know I'm pretty much fucked when Thomas somehow makes his way into the building and into my office, closing and locking my door even before I'm able to make a sound. I stand frozen in place behind my desk, my mind working overtime to find a way out of this scenario. Anyone passing the closed door of my office would assume I'd already made my way down the fire stairs to safety. It's a given, because

I never close my door. This is the exception, so the assumption would be I'm well and I'm safe. Not still standing in my office with a crazed maniac who holds a gun toward me and orders that I don't make a sound, otherwise he'll shoot me.

I'm not afraid for myself. I'm afraid for everyone else. I'm afraid for my father, and what will become of him if I'm no longer here. I'm fearful for Jack, whose heart I'm so entwined with, I don't know that he'll survive this loss. I'm thinking about surviving if only to save everyone else around me from the torment of my death. That's all I can think about as I hold out a hand and motion in a 'steady, steady' manner for Thomas to put the gun down.

He's changed so much that I almost don't recognize him. His eyes are crazed, like he hasn't slept in days, and the stench. God, the stench! He hasn't showered in days, either. His shadow has turned into a full blown growth, now a beard, and I can't understand what's happened to him. Our breakup could not have done this to him; if anything, we were both better off without each other.

"Thomas," I whisper.

"Don't say my name," he whispers, then motions with his gun for me to move to the door. "We're going for a little ride," he says, and we walk to the bank of elevators.

Several minutes have passed, ample time for

everyone to have evacuated the building. We wait at the elevators, and I know in that moment that there is no threat of fire. Thomas did this himself, and he did it to get me on my own. Elevators are not supposed to be used in the event of a fire—he knows this and he's got a phobia for taking unnecessary risks. This is how I know he's the one who's set off the alarms—because he knows it's safe to use the elevator.

He uses the butt of the gun to push me into the lift, where I have to hold my breath as the smell overpowers me in the confined space. I am about to gag when the lift opens in the basement and he leads me to a car and pops the trunk open. I look at him like he's lost his mind. Because he has.

"What's happened to you?" I ask. I need to understand how he's gone from the way he was so impeccably groomed to the way he's so disheveled now.

"Get in," he orders, and I stand there, watching him reluctantly, until he jabs the gun painfully into my side, forcing me to get into the trunk. He closes it and less than a minute later, we're moving. He's speeding through the basement garage and then he's going over a hump and hitting something hard before swerving and driving on. I think I might be sick from the movement, but I suck in a breath and try to stem the tide of emotions running through me as I consider my options. This is one scenario in which I know that there'll be no white knight in shining armor riding in to rescue me. Thomas will make sure of that. If I'm to survive this, I'm going to have to rely on myself and myself alone.

CHAPTER 46

JACK

My lungs are burning as fear spreads throughout my body. It seeps heavily through my bones and puddles in my veins. My breath is short, a stabbing pain radiating where my heart should be. If I lose her now, I don't know what I'll do.

When Olivia's security call me to tell me what's happened, my brain goes into overdrive as I consider all the possibilities of what's happened to her. Unfortunately, I keep coming back to the same one and it's not a good one. I can't get to her office quick enough, and when I do, there are hundreds of people milling about on the street pouring into the roadside. It's like a scene from a movie and I'm expecting that at any minute, I'll wake up and realize it was all just a bad dream.

The fire brigade have declared there was never any sign of a fire, and the alarms were deliberately set off. Something we all know even before they emerge from the building to declare their findings. There could be no other explanation for what happened here today, and no indication as to where Olivia could possibly be. I don't even want to think about the worst-case scenario, but I have to be prepared for anything and everything. No matter how mad it makes me.

Max is frantic as he approaches me, and I don't think I've ever seen a man so distraught. His movements are erratic as he gives me two stilted words then walks back toward the entry of the building. He walks back to me, then turns in a circle as though he could conjure up Olivia's presence. Mentally, the man is gone; he's already checked out, expecting the worst.

"I need you to call your friend at the NYPD," I tell him, taking hold of his lapels. He needs to calm down; I can't have him falling apart on me now. "Get access to the cameras to all exit points; start with the basement. Then they need to search every inch of this building."

"Do you know how many floors this building has?" Max yells at me like I've lost my mind. He's lost the last shred of his mind and I don't think I'll be able to control the narrative much longer if he continues on this path.

"If you have to buy the damn building, you do it," I hiss, walking toward building security, who's deep in conversation with one of my own.

"A woman who was in this building when the emergency alarms kicked in didn't evacuate this building and she's not answering her phone. We need access to her floor now," I tell him.

"There's a process we need to go through to get everyone back in," he tells me, taking his sweet time as he speaks. His attitude is infuriating me as he stands taller and tucks a thumb into each side of his belt.

"Damn your processes. We're talking about a missing woman here."

He doesn't seem impressed with anything I'm saying until Amy sidles up to us and places a hand on the man's arm like they are old friends. She smiles up at him, a dazzling smile that causes her lips to curl up at the sides.

"It's Olivia," she tells the guard. "Olivia's the one that's missing."

He gives me a confused look which quickly morphs into irritation as he springs into action.

"Well, why didn't you say so!" he admonishes, paving the way for me. "Anything else you need, you just come right on back down here and ask."

Amy walks with me as we make our way to the bank of elevators and then up to the level on which The Workshop is located.

"She wouldn't just disappear like this of her own volition," she tells me as we walk together, a crease in her forehead.

"I know she wouldn't," I mutter.

The memory of Olivia's skin against mine last night is the only thing I can think of as my mind races at a million miles an hour. Her arms and legs wrapped around me like she couldn't get close enough. She was never close enough. My throat constricts on a silent scream as I consider all the awful things that could've happened to her. She wouldn't have walked away, there was no chance of that. The more obvious scenario is that she would have been taken by someone. But who would've been able to get close enough undetected? And how?

I'm unable to accept that Olivia is not here. I'm burning up inside as I feel myself losing control of the situation. I cannot lose control. The concept is entirely foreign to me. Knowing and predicting things, being able to determine how well a property will do and the outcome of every step I take. This is what I've based my life's work on. But not knowing where Olivia is and what's happened is tearing me up inside.

Her office is empty. Everything neatly in its place. Down to her handbag, sitting on her chair as though she were getting ready to leave. And there on her desk, like a beacon announcing the end of my world, her phone nestled quietly atop a stack of papers.

"Where is she?"

Max comes running into the room, bracing his outstretched arms on the door frame as he studies us, panic settling deep in his soul. She's not the first thing he sees, so he manifests his pain. The look on our faces must tell him everything he needs to know, because his legs give way and he crumples to the floor unceremoniously. For a man as strong as I know him to be, he's gone down like a sack of potatoes and been reduced to a fragment of his former self. He leans against the wall and sobs his daughter's name over and over again, and I think he's gone into some sort of shock.

"We'll find her," I tell him, crouching to meet his eyes. I feel just as deflated as he looks, but I can't show him any weakness. Not now when he needs me to hold things together. "And when we do, she can't see you like this. So get yourself together and let's go check the cameras."

CHAPTER 47

OLIVIA

There's a lot to be said for making bad choices.

Thomas Thackeray was one of those bad choices.

He was my worst choice.

When he pops the boot and retrieves me, it's all I can do to stop myself from toppling over when he manhandles me and urges me forward. I don't know where we are, but we couldn't have been driving more than forty minutes or so.

When I look at him now, I understand that I never really loved him. Compared to what I have with Jack, what was between Thomas and me could never have been considered love. I marvel at my blind foolishness when everyone around me had warned me but I hadn't listened. That made it all the harder; that everyone could see what I very well couldn't.

The car is left behind as we walk up to an old cabin in the woods. There doesn't seem to be a soul for miles, the only sound the birds chirping and, in the distance, the soft lapping of a stream. I've never been here before, don't know what this place is or even how Thomas would have come across it. But I'm trembling with fear that I'm alone with him out in the middle of nowhere and knowing what he's capable of. Thomas Thackeray doesn't have a merciful bone in his body, and if my history with him is anything to go by, I'm sure he doesn't mean well.

"What are we doing here, Thomas?" I ask him once again, and he sniggers, jabbing the butt of his gun in my side with such viciousness, I know I'm going to bruise. I don't know that it will matter much though, since I'll probably be dead soon.

"You were extremely quiet the whole time we were together," he says, then adds ,"you've become mighty chatty since we've been apart."

I press my lips together at his observation, saying nothing. There was never much to say to a man who was so self-involved, he expected the whole damn world to revolve around him.

"You couldn't just stay away and leave well enough alone, could you?" I hiss at him. If this is going to be my last day on earth, I'm going to get a few things off my chest.

He stops walking and gives me a disgusted look, his expression alone sending daggers through me. How much did he actually hate me?

"Not if it meant your happiness with that imposter, Jack Speed."

He says this so softly, so calmly, I know there is

more to this than just me. This is so much bigger than just his anger at me leaving him.

"That imposter is more man than you'll ever be."

Thomas ignores me and points the gun in my direction, urging me to keep walking. Every step I take toward the old decrepit cabin feels like a death knell. I swallow back my fear and walk, my mind racing at a thousand miles an hour as I assess my surroundings, hoping an opportunity to get away from him will somehow open itself to me. When his phone rings, I watch as he looks down at the screen, then stabs a finger at the device to reject the call and places the phone back in his pocket. He's wearing a beige trench coat that is filthy, and his fingers are grimy like he's been toiling in a garden. I've never known Thomas to have any sort of interest in gardening, so this catches me by surprise. However I soon come to understand just what he'd been doing before he made his way into the city and helped himself into my office.

Just before we reach the rickety steps leading up to the cabin, he guides me toward the back of the house, pushing me in front of him as I struggle down a path through brambles and overgrown weeds. I would have considered the area beautiful had it been well kept. I round the house, Thomas on my heels, and stop short almost at the foot of the porch when I see a shovel strewn in front of the porch stairs leading into the house. And just beyond the shovel, perhaps ten feet away at most, there was a gaping hole in the earth which looked suspiciously like a grave.

Thomas makes no move to push me forward. Instead, he watches me as I stop, the color draining from my face, then turn back to him in question.

"I chose the nicest plot on the property as the site of your burial," he sneers. "I could grant you that, at least."

"You've gone mad."

I utter the words, my eyes never leaving his face. He's gone to extreme lengths to plan this moment, I have no doubt. He's gone to the trouble of digging a grave. He went through security, after executing his well thought out plan to get to me, and now he means to kill me. A shudder passes through my body, creeping up my legs, along my arms, and settling in my head as all hope drains from me. We're in the middle of nowhere, in a place so out of the way, there's probably no way anyone will ever find us. He means to kill me, and he means to do it in a way and in a place where nobody will ever find me.

Thomas sends shivers down my spine when he smiles. He does it with a certain evil that I'm sure couldn't be replicated, even if one tried. It's a certain, knowing smile. He knows what's coming and I don't, and that pleases him immensely. He looks at me like I'm a fool, thinking I've figured it out, when I've done nothing of the sort.

"You'll be pleased to know the grave is big enough for the two of you," he tells me, and his smile morphs into a boyish grin. I'm confused at the meaning of his words; I can't begin to understand what this psychopathic version of Thomas is thinking or planning. But I'm sure I'm going to find out when he waves his gun around theatrically, like he's about to tell me a story.

"Now we wait. When Jack comes for you, I'll make sure you two share one last goodbye with each other before I say my farewell."

"He won't come. I don't mean that much to him."

"You've all but moved in with him, Olivia. How could you not mean anything to him?"

His face clouds with a heart-stopping menace I didn't know he was capable of. So he'd been following me all along. And that is how he knows that Jack and I are together. How could he have gotten past the security guards?

"You won't get away with this," I tell him.

"Oh, but, Olivia," he sighs, somewhat theatrically. "I already have."

CHAPTER 48
JACK

"There!" Amy points at the screen and gasps. I see exactly what she's looking at. The indisputable proof that Thomas Thackeray has abducted Olivia. It can't be a coincidence that he's leaving the building at the same time the fire alarm is blaring and Olivia goes missing.

He wears his hair in a scruffy shag, and his facial hair looks like it hasn't been tended to in months. There's no mistaking the angry glint in his eyes as he maneuvers a car out of the basement and onto the streets of New York. He's driving what appears to be a rental car and Olivia doesn't appear anywhere on the screen, which means he could only have put her in the trunk. I am livid. My face turns to stone, so hard and heavy I could cut through a human with just a glance.

Beside me, I hear a whimper and turn to see Amy with a hand covering her mouth, as though sealing it shut so she doesn't let out what she can no longer hold in. Her face is pale, a mask of terror firmly in place as her body thrums with tension.

There is an inordinate amount of fear shooting through her body, and I can't reconcile this Amy with the one who's usually so calm and collected.

I cut my gaze across to Ainsley, give her a knowing look then shift my eyes to Max. She understands me perfectly and ushers Max into a chair to calm him down as his world starts to collapse around him. I put a hand to Amy's elbow and guide her out of the room, down the hallway until we reach a small office and we slip in quietly.

"What is it?" I ask her.

She shakes her head and refuses to tell me, when I know all she wants to do is confide in me.

"Tell me," I probe.

Her trembling hand falls from her mouth to her side, and she rolls her eyes in defeat, like she'd rather be anywhere else but here in this moment.

"I don't want to think what he'll do to her," she mumbles, grief-stricken. There is an enormous sense of loss in her tone, and I don't want to think about the possibilities running through her head. I already know what Thackeray is capable of. I've known since Luke Mitchell did his deep dive and discovered what Thackeray had been up to during his college days.

The urgency in Amy's voice tells me she either knows about his past, which is highly doubtful, or she knows what he's done to Olivia. I turn this over in my head, mulling it carefully. Olivia never did tell me why she left the country after her break up with her ex fiancé. If anything, she's avoided the topic as though it could contaminate any happiness we might have. The idea that Thackeray could do to Olivia what he's done to other women is not far from my mind. Just the thought of him hurting her in any way severs something deep inside me, a burning fury building up inside me. And then I fall back down to earth with a resounding thud; I can't ponder what may have happened in the past. I need to concentrate on the possibility of what may happen if I don't find Olivia in time.

"You have to find her," she whispers, her desperation tingling my bones. I do have to find her. And I will.

My phone rings as I stalk back down the hallway toward the surveillance room. In my haste to get back to the search, I put the phone to my ear without checking the number, barking my name down the line at the inconvenience of an unwanted call during the unfolding drama.

"I thought you might want proof of life," a male voice rasps down the line. The hairs on the back of my neck bristle as I listen carefully, realizing immediately who it is and knowing these next few minutes will be crucial. I don't even know how he got my number, but I guess I'm not the only resourceful one here.

"Thackeray, what have…"

The bastard cuts me off before I can get a word

in.

"Shh, Shh, shh.." he lets out a rush of requests for quiet, telling me he wants me to listen. "I'm doing you a favor here. Don't you want to hear the lovely Olivia's voice?"

I hold my breath, my answer dying in my lungs. I'm listening to anything and everything I can pick up from this phone call. He's outdoors, which is obvious from the sounds of nature filtering through the background noise. Aside from that, there's not much else I can discern, except that Thackeray seems too calm for such evil. Which concerns me greatly.

"What do you want?" I ask him.

"It's very simple, really," he starts, as though explaining a concept I am unable to grasp. "I'm going to put Olivia on the line to let you know how well I'm treating her. Then you're going to get in your car and drive to a location I give you. Alone. Where the three of us will discuss what went wrong between Olivia and me and how we can right this wrong."

He stops talking long enough for me to register what he's saying. But all I can hear is what he's not saying. Could it be as simple as him giving me their location? When he doesn't continue, I test out my theory.

"That's it? You just want to talk?"

"Just a chat," he confirms. "If I smell even the slightest whiff of anyone else with you, I will put a bullet through her head. You know I'll do it, Jack boy, so don't test me."

I know very well that he'll do it. And he knows that I won't risk Olivia's safety. I'm damn sure he knows it.

"Put Olivia on the phone," I tell him.

There's a pause, some rustling and muffled words in the background and I imagine he's put the phone to his shirt to prevent me from hearing the conversation between him and Olivia.

Amy catches up to me and shoots me a look of consternation. I shake my head slightly, indicating for her not to make a sound.

When Olivia's voice comes on the line, it's all I can do to stop myself reaching into the phone to touch her and pull her to me. Her voice is small, vulnerable, and it's stretching at something fragile in my soul.

"I don't want you to come," is the first thing she says into the phone. I'm sure she already knows that's not an option for me.

"Are you okay?"

I imagine her nodding on the other end of the phone before she speaks again. She's putting on a brave front.

"I'll be fine. Thomas won't hurt me."

I hear the fear in her voice, even though she's trying to be courageous for my sake. My muscles tighten as rage pollutes every vein in my body. I will tear Thackeray limb from limb once I get my hands on him.

"She's right, you know." Thomas chimes as he comes back on the line. "I won't hurt her... until I've got you here to watch."

CHAPTER 49

OLIVIA

I don't know the point where someone crosses from sanity into madness. But I know that's precisely where Thomas is right now. He has lost his mind.

I realize there's nowhere for me to run as he parks himself on the middle tread of the porch steps and watches me where I stand a few meters away. There's nowhere for me to run, and if I dare try, he will simply put a bullet in my back. I'm sure of it.

I decide to take my chances and try for survival. I'll do anything I need to do to stay alive, at least until Jack gets here and I work out a solution where Thomas will be happy and Jack will not get hurt. I know that won't go down well with Jack, but even if I am forced to go back to Thomas, that's a small price to pay in order for Jack to stay safe. The thought of losing him terrifies me. It pulls something stark and raw from deep within me, and I know without a doubt that I couldn't live in a world where Jack did not live.

"We could've had it all, you know," Thomas

whispers, a faraway look in his eyes.

His words repel me. We would've had nothing. And I'm glad things happened the way they did, otherwise I'd probably have married him and been none the wiser. But instead of telling him this, I reverse my emotions in a bid to make him understand where the blame lies.

"We could've had it all," I agree. "But you cheated on me. And you tried to rape me."

"It's not rape if it's between consenting partners."

His words shock me. He's not only mad, but he's also delusional. I can't touch this one without turning him against me, so I fixate on my first point.

"You cheated on me."

"Are you that repulsed that you found me with a man?" he asks, hanging his head. If I didn't know any better, I'd think he was ashamed.

"The gender of who you cheated with is beside the point. The fact of the matter is that you cheated."

He shakes his head emphatically and I realize it doesn't matter what I tell him, he will not accept blame for what happened between us.

"I never meant to hurt you, Olivia."

For a moment, he seems contrite. Apologetic, even. He's aged so much since I last saw him, his eyelids sagging, his skin peeling against a once beautiful face. I can't believe the change in him and how he's gone from having the world at his feet to this monster now standing before me.

"What's past is past," I tell him, perhaps in a way to alleviate him of the burden that lies squarely on his shoulders. "I don't bear you any ill-will."

"You've locked me out of your life."

"That's because we're in the past, Thomas. You did hurt me, and I needed time to heal. I'm still healing."

"With Jack?" he spits.

I realize I don't know what his triggers are. Obviously, Jack is one.

"Jack is a good friend," I tell him, deflecting.

"We were good friends at one time," he reminds me.

"We were. We've known each other a long time, Thomas. I know you wouldn't do anything to hurt me. This is not you."

My voice cracks as I speak, a silent plea. I don't know what to do to turn this situation around.

"I became a different person after you," he tells me.

"Everybody changes, Thomas. That's not always a good thing."

Definitely not in his case. His change was far beyond anything I ever anticipated. In fact, it was the worst thing that could've happened. He was the worst thing that could've happened to me. I don't tell him that.

"I became what I am because of you."

His voice cracks. Momentarily, he has reverted to what I imagine he would have been like as a little boy. Broken and vulnerable. In need of reassurance. And I know it's only our shared past that softens my heart toward him, making me feel sorry for him. But I can't. I can't let him have that effect on me. The man is holding a gun on me and he will not hesitate to use it. With the flip of a switch, Thomas could kill me as calmly as he would comb his hair. I would know; I've seen that side of him.

"It's not too late for you to walk away from this, Thomas," I reassure him. "Just let me go and go on with your life like none of this ever happened."

"So you can go on with yours?"

He's resentful as he hisses, his accusatory tone menacing as his spittle flies through the air. He becomes so agitated when the thought of Jack and me together crosses his mind.

We're interrupted by the sound of his phone as it chirps in his pocket. He looks down at it then reads aloud.

"Jack's here," he tells me, holding the phone to his ear. He speaks into the receiver. "Did you come alone?" A pause, then 'come around the back.' He hangs up and gives me what I can only describe as a smile bereft of all humanity. Thomas has well and truly gone over the edge.

"On your knees," he says, stepping down from

the stairs and coming towards me. I flounder, hesitating, afraid of what's to come. I'm right next to the hole in the ground and I'm afraid. "On your knees," he repeats, and he pushes me down until I'm on my knees facing the makeshift grave. Thomas stands behind me, and I feel the muzzle of the gun as it presses into the back of my head. He's going to kill me, and he wants Jack to watch. He wants him to suffer.

I see Jack just as he turns the bend and comes into view, walking towards us. He's alone, and he's wearing a suit. He looks larger than life, but that could just be the view from where I'm kneeling on my knees. He is a looming behemoth and I am a wilting flower as he edges closer until Thomas orders him to stop where he is.

"Let her go," Jack starts, his assessing gaze raking over me for any sign of injury before he flicks his attention to Thomas. "Let her go and we can talk about this like two grown men, just you and me."

Thomas scoffs. "I used to be a man. Until I wasn't."

CHAPTER 50

JACK

I've never been more thankful for anything in my life. The fact that Olivia is alive and breathing, if a little worse for wear, fills my heart with hope. But her position on the ground, under the executioner's sword, gives rise to a mounting pressure in my head. I don't know what I'll do if he hurts her, which he obviously plans to do. I need to buy us some time, something I know is a precious commodity given the current state of our positions.

My eyes find Olivia's, and it's all I can do to stop myself from falling to the ground and embracing her. There is so much fear in her eyes, and a plea. She didn't want me here, and now my presence has just added to her fear.

"Don't even think about it," Thomas rasps. "Eyes on me."

I swing my eyes his way, stand to my full height, and fix my expression to one that could cut through concrete. If this was happening, it would happen on my terms. And I understood exactly what it was that made Thomas tick. The whole reason he had latched onto Olivia. The engagement he sprang on her out of nowhere; how he orchestrated it knowing she'd never be the one to leave him or destroy her good public standing. He'd seen a weakness in the beautiful but vulnerable Olivia Kane, and he'd played on it, milking the situation for all it was worth.

"Name your price," I tell him, throwing that gauntlet down. Everybody has a price. I wanted to see how cheap he was.

"I'm not buying," he disputes.

"Everybody's buying. If the price is right."

"You couldn't give me anywhere near what I would have gotten had I married her."

I hear Olivia's sharp intake of breath, register the shame and hurt as they cross her face, but can't do anything to comfort her. He used her for his own purposes, for his own personal gain. If anything, she should know that he never loved her—he was just stringing her along because of what he would have gained from a union between them. I needed her to see the ugly side of him. I needed to put this to bed and get Thackeray out of our lives once and for all so we could move on.

"I can give you more than you can imagine," I tell him, and I know I've hit the jackpot, because his ears seem to perk up.

"She's worth so much more than you've got."

"And I'm willing to do whatever it takes to give you whatever you want. Tell me what you want,

Thackeray. What's it going to take to get us all on the same page, hmmm?"

I know I sound more confident than I feel. Olivia swings her head in my direction, surprise in her eyes. I don't know what she's surprised by—the faux confidence I'm exuding or the fact that I would do anything to save her. She sways on her knees and I cock my head in a show of support, telling her not to fall apart on me now. I hope she's read my message correctly; I need her strong and capable for what comes next.

"Everything was fine until you came along," Thackeray hisses, his anger resurfacing with a vengeance. It seems he wants to drag this out as long as he possibly can. Wants to point fingers and lay blame where there is none. He's the master of his own demise. But he obviously doesn't see it that way.

"My timing is probably lousy," I agree with him. "But we need to find a middle ground here."

"My middle ground is to be rid of the both of you."

It takes everything in me not to lunge at him when he presses the gun into the crevice between Olivia's shoulders. Internally, I start to shut down, pure unadulterated rage flowing through my veins. But I can't allow myself to show him any emotions that could possibly point to my Achilles heel. Olivia is my weakness. She's impaled herself upon my heart in a way that assures me there'll never be another like her.

"Why don't you lower your gun before you do something there's no coming back from."

"I won't rest a day until I've destroyed you both," he sneers.

"In doing that, you're destroying yourself. We all go down," I tell him. "You won't get anything out of either of us. And you will spend the rest of your days in a prison cell."

I feel it's necessary to remind him of this. I don't know where exactly his head is at, but it can't be somewhere good. I've already taken the necessary steps to ensure that if anything happens to either of us, he will carry out the rest of his days in misery, if not in a coffin.

"Stop talking," he rasps. He is conflicted as his hand wavers and his eyes start to shoot about the forest around us. We are cocooned in a deathly silence; even the birds have stopped chirping and the quiet is pervasive out in the middle of nowhere.

"Tell me what it is you want." I need to keep him talking, but this only seems to anger him, because he clenches his teeth then stretches his lips back the way a tiger would if about to pounce on its prey.

"Stop. Talking."

I know I've gone as far as I can with the conversation and clamp my mouth shut, willing my own silence as I slide my eyes toward Olivia.

She pleads with me silently, and I understand it's because she probably thinks her ex is more likely to hurt me than to hurt her. In some ways, she probably feels responsible that she's brought Thackeray into my life. But I don't hold her responsible. I couldn't. If anything, I'm grateful that she's in my life, even with all the baggage that is part of her history. I just don't want to see her get hurt, and I'm going to make damn sure that doesn't happen.

CHAPTER 51

OLIVIA

So this is what death looks like.

Anyone that tells you death doesn't have a smell is lying. I smell it and I feel it. I even taste it. Just as sure as Thomas is standing behind me with a gun aimed at my head.

There are those that tell you, after their near-death experiences, that you see your life flash before your eyes, soundless, like a movie reel playing your life in reverse. But I beg to differ. There are no flashbacks, no movie reels, no black and white cinematic playing in the background. There's no time for that. How much could you possibly cram into a couple of minutes when you have more than a quarter of a century's worth of life behind you? All your memories, your experiences... there's no way they could all be reduced to just a few fleeting minutes. It's impossible.

Anyone that tells you death has no meaning is lying. That's all I can think as the smoking gun is lowered and I start to fall. Falling in slow motion, though never quite landing.

There is a great big fire in my chest and I feel the burning. There is a metallic taste in my mouth, the distinct flavor of blood.

And two of the most distinct memories from my childhood—my mother, young beautiful and alive, telling me that everyone has a story to tell—how good the story is depends on the storyteller. I imagine the story I'll tell her when we meet again.

And my father advising me, "Don't ever, ever in your life trust anyone, Olivia. Trust no one." That's the first life-lesson he taught me. And there I was, trusting Thomas and letting him into my life. I let him corner me into an unwanted marriage. I let him run my life and make my decisions for me. And eventually, he hurt me physically, almost destroying me. Why had I not been able to see what everyone else could see?

That's all I could remember from my life as my body finally hit the ground and my eyes bulged at the sickening pool of blood enveloping my body.

So much blood. It's everywhere, a deep crimson red. Warm liquid is coating my hands as blindness finds my eyes.

So this is what death looks like… I wait for death to take me. I welcome it even. It would be so much easier to just let go. To simply fade into the background and cease to be. Some might mourn me. Others may not. But at least I would have died knowing I was loved. Knowing I loved. Safe in the knowledge that Thomas can't hurt me anymore. He can never hurt me again. He's done that already. He took my sanity and then he took my life.

Jack. My eyelids soar open, then shutter again. In the distance, I can hear the faint sound of Jack calling my name. He seems so far away. He is far away. At least he's okay. I fear for him, the thought of him blaming himself for what's happened here today. I need him to know that none of this was his fault. Having him come here and risk his own life for me tells me everything I need to know. Jack loved me as much as I loved him. I wish I had told him while I was still on earth. I wish I had let him know whilst my tongue was heavy with words. I had known, but I had been too afraid to tell him, out of fear that I would scare him off. Too much, too soon. But it was somehow not enough and not soon enough. I never should have waited.

He's calling my name over and over again, and suddenly there are hands on me, shaking me awake, turning me over, holding my head. I feel the steady thump of a heart underneath my chest. I think he's holding me to his chest as the life seeps out of me. His voice is pleading with me to wake up, and I hear chatter. The chatter of many different voices around me, some familiar and some not. I'm sure I've finally arrived where I'm supposed to be.

There is a light shining behind my eyelids. Like the light at the end of the tunnel, I believe.

Someone is squeezing my hand. I wonder if my mother will be the first one I see as I cross over to the other side. I'm so overwhelmed. I'm excited by the possibility of seeing her again, but I'm saddened at all that I'll be leaving behind. At everyone I'll be missing. All the beautiful people in my life who have been there from the start.

My death is going to break my father's heart. He never recovered after mother passed, and I'm his last breathing relation, his only child. I don't know how he's going to go on without me. I hope he can finally find comfort in Ainsley's arms. I don't know why those two never got together, but I know they're going to need each other to pull through this one. I pray they do the right thing and stay close to one another in their time of need.

And Amy. My dear poor Amy. I have no words. She sacrificed her own life to stay beside me through my darkest hours. Closer than sisters, I can't even think how she's going to function without a limb. Because in effect, that's what we were to one other... an essential limb which we could not possibly survive without.

My name is wafting on the breeze, an echo from the distance. A scream, and then sobbing. I hear it all, and Jack as he brushes my hair back from my face, murmuring for me to come back to him. I know it's him because I'd know those hands anywhere. I'd know that scent anywhere.

And as the dull thud of life bleeds out of me, my eyes shutter and I spurt one last breath.

My last thought is about how I'll be haunting Thomas from the grave for the term of his natural life.

CHAPTER 52

JACK

"Fainted?"

I laugh. I've never been so happy to see Olivia's confused face. I watch her carefully as she rubs at her temple and looks at me, bewildered. Her clothes are drenched in blood and when she looks down at herself, she goes so pale that I think she's going to faint again.

"Oh my God," she whispers, scrunching up her face. Her bloody hand shakes as she pulls it away from her shirt.

"You're okay," I tell her, smoothing her hair away from her face.

"But I felt the bullet hit me. I felt the fire in my chest. I died."

She argues with me as though it's what she wished for, and I can't help but laugh and shake my head. I hold my hand out to her and tell her it's time to leave. She asks me about Thomas, and I look over my shoulder at his body as it lays by the grave he had dug for someone else but which came to be his final resting place. Someone has been quick to action and covered his body with a sheet. I turn away quickly and urge Olivia's gaze back to me as I lead her to the front of the house, explaining what happened.

The trauma of what transpired here today will stay with us for a little while. I know this. But it's nothing we can't overcome and get past. Eventually we'll forget and we'll go on. And if we don't, that's what good therapists are for. I've seen a lot in my life, but it's Olivia that I'm worried about. I don't have any idea how she is going to fare through all of this, not after having a loaded gun held to her head.

"You didn't die. You're still here with me." I wrap an arm around her waist and pull her into my side, thankful that things went just the way we planned.

"What happened?"

"Thackeray told me to come alone. In theory, I did. I had some of my men come through the other end of the forest, sneaking up without him noticing. They did nothing until it seemed like Thackeray was agitated enough to do something to hurt you. That's when they shot him."

"So much blood." She looks down at her shirt again. I have to get her out of her clothes a soon as possible.

"Thackeray fell on top of you, that's why there's blood all over you. And the impact of him falling on you, combined with the gunshots, may have seemed like you were the one getting shot. I'm just glad you weren't hurt."

◆ ◆ ◆

I strip her clothes off her and bundle them in a bag to be disposed of with our household waste. I never want to see those clothes again, and I never want to be reminded of what happened today and how I almost lost her. I walk Olivia into the shower. It's there that she breaks down, her shoulders quaking as she releases heavy sobs into the mist of steam swirling around us. I hold her close to me, smoothing down her hair, letting her sobs escape in what I know is a cleansing process that has to happen. Today she buried the last remnants of her past with Thackeray. Tomorrow, she'll be able to move on with me and I will make sure that there will be no remembrance of the man that almost cost me the love of my life.

Her sobbing subsides, but she doesn't make a move to leave my open arms. Instead, I pull away, picking up the shampoo and lathering it into her hair. I rinse her hair out, take extra care with the body wash all over her body, and pay attention to her well-being. My only thought is to take care of her. The only way I can do this is by worshipping her body, my temple. When the fragrance of honey and jasmine fills the bathroom and she's clean, I wrap a towel around her body and another around her head.

"I want you to rest for a while," I tell her, pulling back the bedsheets for her. "I have a few phone calls to make and then I'll come and join you."

"Don't leave me," she whispers, her eyelids heavy with sleep. She's absolutely exhausted after the day she's had.

"Never."

◆ ◆ ◆

Olivia sleeps throughout the afternoon and well into the night. Her father, Amy and Ainsley all come past to check up on her and breathe a sigh of relief when they ensure she is indeed well and asleep in her room.

"I haven't had a chance to thank you for saving Olivia," Max tells me, as I walk him to the door.

"There's no need for thanks," I tell him. "Anyone would have done the same."

"No." He shakes his head and gives me a thoughtful look. "Not everyone would have done the same. I can see why she's in love with you."

I raise my eyebrows in surprise. This is news to me. Olivia has never so much as uttered the words, and I find I'm surprised that her father is the one enlightening me. Max just smirks and gives me a pointed look, wondering how I could be so daft.

"I can't imagine she would have been as open

with her feelings as a girl is expected to be," he explains. "The thing with He Who Shall Not Be Named really left its mark on her. I don't think it was easy for her to consolidate her emotions in a meaningful way after their break up."

"You don't need to explain anything to me."

"I don't," he agrees. "But I think you should know. She may be too scared to let you in, but I hope you're persistent."

And that right there is Max's approval in a nutshell. He isn't the type to come right out and say it, but I understand the gist of what he is saying, and I'm glad that we have had this chat. It tells me everything I need to know about what Max is thinking and where my relationship with Olivia should be heading. I know he never approved of Olivia's ex; he never even liked the guy. So this is everything.

Before he steps into the elevator to leave, Max puts a hand to my shoulder and squeezes. A support of sorts. And he leaves me standing in the foyer of my own home, his daughter quietly sleeping in a room beyond, my thoughts concentrated on what I need to do next.

CHAPTER 53
JACK

"It's time," I say, leading Olivia across the threshold of my apartment and into the second apartment I purchased to turn one whole level into my home. I've been holding onto these properties for a few years now, an investment I made that fell by the wayside when I couldn't find a reason to spend any length of time in New York. Now I hoped the investment would finally pay off as I put it to use.

"Time for what?"

I pause for a moment and look down at the card in my hand, before swiping it through the reader and pushing the door open. She hasn't been into this apartment before. It's completely empty, and an abundance of light is filtering through the windows. It sits at a different angle to the other suite, so this one is airier, lighter. And it takes her breath away. The same way it did for me the first time I saw it.

"It's empty," she breathes.

"A blank slate."

I look at her. I want a clean slate with her. A

blank canvas. I want the world with her. And I want it forever.

"What are you going to do with it?"

She's transfixed as she walks to the window and looks out. She's giving me just the reaction I want, and I hope we're headed in the right direction as I go and stand beside her, looking out at the world below us. We're so high up, but how much higher can we go, I wonder?

"I'm moving to New York," I tell her.

We may have shared a few nights together, but nothing was designed past that. There was no label to what we had together, even though I was more than happy to assign one.

She gasps, swinging her head in my direction. This was not what she was expecting. I think we'd always known there was an expiry date on my time here in New York. So this comes as a massive surprise to her. But not to me. It's time I made the move. For my business, it's the logical next step. And for me on a personal level—there's nowhere else I'd rather be.

"Permanently? Will you live here?"

"I need to find myself a good designer first."

I laugh and she scoffs.

"I want you to be the one that designs this space for me, Olivia. I want to open it up to the other apartment and I want one expansive space to live in."

"So much space," she whispers. One person

could never need that much space. Two people couldn't even.

"Olivia..." I start then stop. There's so much I want to tell her. So much I want to say. But I'm not exactly sure where to start. This is a new playing field for me, and I'm afraid to stuff it up. But then again, she's all I've ever wanted. And I don't intend on losing her. If I stuff it up, I'll just have to go back and fix it again, I realize.

Olivia waits patiently as I look down, then shuffle my feet awkwardly before looking back up at her again. The light throws a halo around her head, my angel, and she looks right at home where she's standing. She puts a hand to her hip and is the picture of perfection as she smiles up at me.

"I'm excited to tackle this project," she says, rubbing her palms together gleefully. "I've never designed such a huge space for one man only."

I'm quiet as her words sink in. If it were any other woman, I'd say she was fishing for an invitation. But not Olivia. Her mind doesn't work that way. She comes out and says exactly what's on her mind. If she wanted to know if I'd be sharing the space with anyone, she'd simply ask.

"I won't be the only one living here, Olivia," I tell her, walking around the room in circles. She's silent, a question in her eyes as she watches me move back and forth across the floor.

"Do you have any ideas for the space?"

I approach her with a few slow steps and tuck a strand of loose hair behind her ear. Our eyes connect and our souls do that silent thing they do when they're in the same room. "I want you to design a space for me," I tell her. "For my family." I rest my hand against her hair, and I feel nothing but anxious knots in my stomach as I watch for her reaction. Her face is blank and I can't tell what she's thinking. "For my wife. And my children when they come," I continue.

I hear the gasp of her breath catching as she continues to stare at me. She's surprised and confused and perhaps she has some idea of what I'm saying but she's unsure. I move my hand away from her and let my arms drop to my sides. The very thought of living without her causes the monster inside me to rear its ugly head.

She doesn't say anything for the longest time, and I wonder if she's gone into shock. If someone had told me last year this is where I'd be at this point in time—standing before the love of my life and struggling with how to ask her to marry me, I'd have laughed. There's no way anyone, least of all me, could have seen this coming.

"Say something." When she looks back at me blankly, I lift her hand to my lips and kiss the back, never removing my eyes from her face. "I think I fell in love with you the minute you ran into me in the park that first day we met." I pause and give her a meaningful look. She licks her lips and inhales deeply. The rest of my life hangs on the balance of what she does next. "I want to spend the rest of my life with you and I want to do it here."

CHAPTER 54

OLIVIA

My mind is running at a hundred miles an hour as I listen to Jack. I have to blink repeatedly, mentally pinching myself to make sure I'm not dreaming. The proof of our love for one another lays in what he was willing to do to save me when Thomas kidnapped me. And the way he was the last thing I thought about as I believed the last shred of life was seeping out of me. I love him, perhaps even more than life itself. And I want him to know that, but the words just won't come. Instead, I stand in front of him like a stunned mullet, my body unmoving and my mind in shock. It's not that I don't want this. It's that I want it too much, and I'm too afraid to get ahead of myself and jinx my future.

"Marry me," he says.

Two words that couldn't be said any simpler, but the answer lodges in my throat as my heart races out of its crevice and I'm incapable of sound. Instead, I nod my head, a smile splitting the sides of my face as I hurl myself at him, winding my legs around his waist. He twirls me around and around the room, his happiness mirroring my own, and I've never felt so complete in my life.

This is the exact opposite of what happened with Thomas, and I'm thankful for that. Jack has given me a choice, and I'm making my own decision. I'm so happy as everything falls into place, and I know... I just know, that everything's going to be okay. I couldn't have conjured a better ending for us if I'd dreamed it up myself.

"Mrs. Jack Speed," I laugh.

"Gable," he corrects. "Mrs. Jack Gable. As in Kane and Gable."

I love this side of him. The side that is light and fun and humorous. It's not often I've seen it as he's tended to his business, but I can see it shining through his personality and I love it. I love everything that he is, and everything that we will be together.

"Were you serious about children?" I stop laughing and look at him seriously as he sets me down on my feet. The words are barely out of my mouth before he has sealed his lips to mine, hungrily delving into the heart of me.

"I was serious about every word I said. I want to have as many children as you're willing to give me."

◆ ◆ ◆

"What, no ring?" Ainsley gives us both a stern

look as she spies my ring finger.

"I didn't want to get ahead of myself," Jack says, putting an arm around my shoulder. "We're going ring shopping tomorrow."

We've invited our nearest and dearest out to dinner to announce our news and to celebrate, even though I disagreed with Jack's idea and told him it was a little premature. He'd told me he wanted our loved ones to know before anyone else did, and I couldn't begrudge him that.

"Well, ring or no ring," my father says, lifting his glass in a toast. "I for one couldn't be happier to welcome Jack into the fold. I hope you live a long and happy life together… and give me many grandchildren."

We all start laughing, and I can't remember the last time I was this happy. I truly can't. And Amy reminds me of this as Jack and my father fall deep into conversation and she tells me how happy she is over my engagement. Although she insists that she saw it coming.

We're discussing rings and dress designs when someone calls out my name, and I turn in my chair to see Gabe McFadden standing beside me. I rise to greet him, smiling and kissing his cheek, surprised yet happy to run into him here. Suddenly, I feel self-conscious about Gabe's closeness to me, and I turn to look at Jack, who smiles and rises to put his hand in Gabe's as I make the introductions.

I'm taken aback by my own reticence to be speaking to Gabe, my own fear of reprimand. And I realize I have a long way to go in undoing the damage Thomas did to me. He wouldn't even allow me to say Gabe's name, let alone greet an old friend in this way. Eventually, I had distanced myself from Gabe just to keep the peace with Thomas. Even though he had been my discovery. I'd met him one day a few years ago as I was running through Central Park. He'd been painting a landscape—apparently a hobby of his—and I'd been mesmerized by the beauty he captured on the canvas and struck up a conversation with him. I'd been the one to convince him to sell some of his work. I'd introduced him to some friends that worked at art galleries and he'd eventually had his own showing. From there, things just seemed to sky-rocket for the artist. I'd met Gabe even before I met Thomas, and our relationship had always been platonic, but for some reason I couldn't understand, Thomas had never taken a liking to the man.

Jack however, is nothing like Thomas. He is already deep in conversation with the artist, his hand still firmly tucked in the other man's as he tells Gabe he's a fan of his work. This makes me love and appreciate Jack even more. And even more so when he insists that Gabe join us for dinner. I watch the two men as they interact. Gabe is Irish born and came to America as a toddler, although he's managed to retain the heavy Irish lilt of his ancestors. He has a head of wide golden brown ringlets and green eyes that are truly stunning. He's handsome in that roguish way artists frequently are, and I know he's broken many a girl's heart in the past. I also know that he recently went through a very bad breakup with his girlfriend and swore off women for a while.

That's why I'm confused when Gabe keeps darting his eyes in interest toward the table, and I look around, trying to see what's got him so worked up. Amy is sitting there watching him, her jaw literally hitting the floor. And when I say literally, I mean well and truly. I nudge her until her chin falls off her hand and she snaps back down to the real world before Gabe takes his leave with a promise for us to catch up soon.

'Well, I guess we'll be seeing him sooner rather than later," Jack says, shooting Amy an arrogant smile. He raises his eyebrows and dabs at the corner of his mouth, his playful side emerging again. "You might want to wipe your mouth, Amy. You have a bit of drool right there."

EPILOGUE:
JACK

Olivia looks resplendent in her ivory gown, a simple body-hugging number that stretches across every necessary curve of her body. She's the most beautiful woman I've ever seen, and I can't get enough of her. I can't stop staring when she doesn't know I'm looking. When she sleeps, I pull up a chair and watch the soft lift and fall of her chest, memorizing every movement she makes.

I've fallen for her in a way that defies belief, and my fascination with her is bordering on obsession, but I can't help it. Today, she's finally mine in mind, body and soul. And on paper. I made sure everyone would know she's taken when I bought her the biggest diamond I could possibly find. A huge diamond in the shape of a teardrop, which she insisted was too big, too flashy, too everything. But I had insisted that she tone down everything else but keep the massive rock. It was the one thing I wouldn't concede defeat to. I needed everyone to know she was mine.

When Olivia throws the bouquet into the small crowd—we'd opted for a very small, intimate wedding with twenty-five guests between us—Amy catches it. I watch as a blush rises up the young woman's neck and don't miss the glance she throws across the room towards Gabe. They've been exchanging furtive glances all afternoon, and I know I'm not wrong in thinking that a storm is brewing between them. Although I'd welcome a relationship between them, Amy has become like a little sister to me, and I don't want to see her get hurt. Something I've already made clear to Gabe on the occasions that he's joined us for dinner or at social gatherings, of which there are few. I know that Gabe recently went through a very nasty break-up, and I also know that he carries a lot of baggage from that bad relationship. I don't want any of that mess to touch Amy in any way, so I'll be watching the development of that relationship very closely.

After we say our goodbyes, we climb into the limousine, and I hit the privacy screen between us and the driver as he heads to the airport to our waiting jet. I can't wait to be on the plane to get my hands on my wife, so I'm on her in a heartbeat, bearing down as my lips find hers and my hand moves up her thigh, lifting her dress. My tongue melds with hers, and she moans into my mouth as I smooth my hand up and down her thigh, then press the tiny mound between her legs. This gets me more than a moan, and she's hungry and tormented, a panting mess as she bites my lip and draws blood. Olivia can be crazy in bed when she wants to be.

"Time for our flight, wife," I murmur into her mouth, as the car comes to a stop on the tarmac. She gives me a disgruntled look then folds the fabric of her dress down to her ankles.

"Time for the rest of our life, husband."

EPILOGUE:
OLIVIA

Jack comes up from behind and winds his arms around my waist, pulling me to him as he nuzzles my neck.

"God, would you stop it already!" I laugh. "You've already done enough!"

His hands move to my stomach, massaging the bump as he is so prone to doing these days. Straight off the mark, he had insisted that we let things happen organically, so naturally, we hit the ground running and got pregnant on our honeymoon. It's five months later and the bump I have is barely discernible under the clothes I wear, but he still knows it's there, and he feels the need to remind me every minute of the day.

"I can't help it if I can't get enough of you," he tells me, nuzzling deeper. "These pregnancy hormones are doing crazy things to Jack Junior."

"You're crazy, you know that?"

I smile and turn in his arms, looking up at his face. I find him more handsome with each day that passes. I wrap my arms around his neck and watch him as he splays his hands against my stomach, connecting with our daughter.

"She's going to be as beautiful as her mother is," he tells me. "Hopefully not as headstrong or stubborn. I'll accept beautiful." He says this matter-of-factly, and I can't help but laugh.

These have been the happiest five months of my life, and if they're any indication, I'm going to have a beautiful life with Jack. He spoils me. In the way he treats me, and they way he takes care of me. His little surprise visits to the office with a picnic hamper. Or the surprise weekend when we flew to Martha's Vineyard for a romantic getaway. His hands are magic as he gives me back rubs when the swell of pregnancy back pain gets too much. And his attentiveness whenever I speak, like he shuts out the whole world and hears only me. He does hear only me. And he makes me feel loved and cherished and adored.

"I need to put the finishing touches on dinner," I tell him, breaking away. He's insistent and pulls me back to him, his fingers trailing down the side of my face in anticipation. He's got that lust filled look in his eyes again. "God, not again," I moan.

"You're insatiable," he murmurs, burying his face in my neck. "And we have more than enough time before our guests arrive."

◆ ◆ ◆

Life doesn't get much better than this. I have my family and friends gathered around me, showering us with congratulations and well wishes. If I didn't know any better, I'd say that they're more excited now they know I'm having a girl than when we told them I was pregnant.

Ainsley holds my cheek in her hands and gives me a wistful look, her eyes shimmering with unshed tears.

"Your mother would be so proud of the woman you've become." She chokes back a sob, and I know she misses her. Just as much as I do. Ainsley has been able to fill that void for me, the one my mother left behind when she passed, but I know that Ainsley herself has felt deep sorrow for the loss of her best friend over the years.

I squeeze Ainsley's hand in mine and give her a small smile before she turns away, trying to stem the tears that threaten to escape.

"Where's Amy?" Jack asks, coming to stand beside me. I give him a puzzled look, then frown as I look around the room. She's nowhere to be seen, and neither is Gabe.

"I don't know. It's not like her to be late."

He looks at my face, registers the worry I now feel, then tells me she's probably just running late and should be here soon.

"What can I get my beautiful wife?" he asks, kissing my forehead.

"You've already given me the world."

"I mean to eat. We can't have Ava going hungry," he says.

"Ava?" I raise my brows and wait for an explanation.

"I think it's a beautiful name. And what could be a more fitting tribute than naming our daughter after your mother?"

My heart softens at his words, tears threatening to escape my eyes.

"Then Ava it is," I tell him, as he folds a hand into my own. "Ava Jackson Gable."

Catch up with Jack and Olivia as Amy and Gabe's story unfolds in "Never Tear Us Apart"

CHAPTER 1 - AMY

And my universe went bang. At the bottom of a mug full of golden, rich syrup.

"Another?"

The waiter smirks, the look on his face telling me everything I need to know. Drinking endless cups of lattes was not going to get me drunk enough to forget. No, that would never happen.

"I've had enough, don't you think?"

I straighten and shoot him a pointed look, like I am the adult trying to sort out my own drunk self. Except, I am anything but. I may have been a little tipsy on chai, but that was about it.

"Come on, kiddo. It's not that bad," he coos.

"You would think so," I stammer. You didn't get dumped on a Friday night because your boyfriend had to go 'find himself.'

He holds up two fingers to indicate his point. "One, I do not have a boyfriend. And two, I wouldn't consider him going on an African safari any form of 'finding himself.'"

If it's at all possible, I straighten even further. "So that was just an excuse he used?"

"Hold up. I did not say that, Ames. I said the guy's not worth his weight in salt if he felt he had to 'go find himself' without you. And in Africa, of all places."

I smile as I look up at him; Martin's said just the right thing at the right time, and it's exactly what I need to hear. I've heard it multiple times, but I can't get past Tatum just up and leaving me. It was so sudden, so far out of left field after seven months of a steady relationship that I was continuously second guessing whether or not I'd read the relationship right. I'd felt sure that we were headed towards an engagement, but instead he surprised me with the announcement that he'd be traveling and he thought we should take a break and see other people.

"That's exactly what Jack and Olivia tell me."

"Well, you'd better listen to them; seems like they know what they're talking about."

I'm glad for these precious little moments after the lunch rush when the coffee shop is dwindling in numbers and I can have a few enlightening moments with Martin. He has a way of making me feel better with a minimal number of words, and I love that about him.

"Olivia hasn't been in here in a while. How is old faithful, anyway?" Martin swipes a cloth across the table, and I recognize this for what it is. Force of habit. The man simply can't sit still. I'd known him ever since he'd come to work at the little coffee shop around the corner from work, and I could safely say that was his signature move. He was never without a tablecloth in his hand.

"She asked for take-out so she could get some work done. Oh shoot, I totally forgot her coffee order!" I slide out of my chair and walk towards the counter as Martin laughs and shakes his head at me. He cherishes these moments just as much as I do.

"You want another?" he asks, knowing the answer even before I open my mouth to speak. I'm a coffee addict by trade, and I'm pretty sure Martin would feed me the liquid gold through a drip if I asked him to. He sets the two cups in a holder and pushes it toward me with a smile. I really love this man.

"You're a godsend," I remind him, winking as I turn hurriedly to leave the coffee shop and head back in to work.

I'm juggling my bag, my phone and the coffee tray as I leave the shop and run smack bang into a brick wall. Well, not really, but it felt like it. Everything in my hands goes crashing against a monster of a man, then tips precariously until the coffee has become intimate with both of our clothes and the floor, and my phone lies in a shattered heap on the ground.

"Oh no," I murmur, turning angry eyes toward the man who stands transfixed, looking at me in surprise.

CHAPTER 2 - GABE

The woman is looking at me like she could pull my hair out. Or gouge my eyes. Maybe both. Her angry face is so endearing, it makes the sides of my mouth curl in a lop sided grin. Her furious gaze rakes over me in disbelief before she looks down at the mess at her feet and shakes her head in annoyance. The waiter runs to her side with a cloth and he's soon joined by another waitress with a mop as they start to clean around her.

"Martin, I'm so…" she starts, but he cuts her off with a hand on her arm and tells her not to apologize. He guides her over to a chair and tells her he'll make a fresh brew, and she takes her seat, stunned at what's happened, before she notices the great big wet patch at the front of her white shirt. I see it at the same time, and for some reason I cannot comprehend, my eyes will not move from her soaked shirt which now clings to her body like a second skin. She looks up to see me staring, and her anger is instantly ramped up. She leaps out of her chair and comes up in my face, waving her finger around in admonishment.

"Do you make it a habit of running into people and creating such mayhem?" she asks, glaring at me.

"Well, no, it's not a habit, but I've been known to be a klutz at times," I tell her, but my humor is lost on her because she stomps her feet and whirls away from me, facing the male waiter who's working at the counter and watching us with amused interest.

"Martin, I need to get home to change," she says to him. "Can I use the phone to call Ollie, please?" She looks down at her tattered phone, her look one of desolation.

"I'll run the coffee over," he tells her.

"You go home and get changed. Do you want me to order you an Uber?"

"Yes please," she murmurs, the softest she's been since I've run into her. She fixes me with a scathing look then turns away again, ignoring me.

"Look, I do apologize for running into you. That was not my intention."

"Noted," she says, without looking at me. Her small frame is minuscule next to my much taller, fuller figure. I can safely say the weight on me is all muscle from hours of working out and training at the gym. I look like a giant next to her.

I step to the side and give the waiter my order as she waits for the Uber to arrive. She has her head bent as she fumbles with her phone, trying in vain to get some sort of heartbeat out of it. I can't help but watch her, admire the elegant curve of her neck and the way her blonde hair just scrapes past her shoulders. When she looks up at the waiter again, I'm mesmerized by her blue-grey eyes, two dazzling pinpoints that I could definitely get lost in. I'm not searching for anyone or anything, and I'm not in a place where I can comfortably embark on a relationship with a woman, but I can't help but be drawn to this person I've never met before. As though we have met before. As though I was meant to be here today, at this time and in this place, to run into her and share this tragically comical moment with her.

"I'd be happy to pay for your dry-cleaning," I tell her, if for no other reason than my desire to have a conversation with her. And to pay for the damage I caused her. That too.

"There's no need," she bites back.

"I insist."

"Let him pay for your dry-cleaning, Amy. It'll make you feel better," the waiter pipes up.

Amy. I let her name slide off my tongue silently. It rather rolls. Right where it belongs. And I can't help but feel how the name absolutely suits her.

"There really is no need," she says, from in between clenched teeth. She's still not over the mess I've made, and it's all I can do to stop myself from laughing at her continued fury.

"I absolutely insist," I tell her. When she shoots me a look that is meant to maim, or maybe kill, I relent and revert to silence in a bid to keep the peace. I don't need to make this any worse than it is.

"What'll you have?" The waiter finally asks me, as the waitress grabs Amy's order and heads out the door.

"Can I at least get you a coffee while you wait for your Uber?" I ask her, and for a moment, her face lights up, as though I've given her the world. The girl is a coffee aficionado, a woman after my own heart. But just a quickly, she realizes her misstep and reverts back to her exasperated scowl, which she directs my way. I take that to mean no.

"Your Uber's here," the waiter tells her, looking down at an alert on his phone.

"Thank you Martin, please put it on my tab," she says, and with a royal flourish, she lifts her chin nonchalantly and heads for the door and out of my life.

CHAPTER 3 - AMY

I can't believe this asshole. He's been at the coffeeshop three days running, and it's as though he's materialized out of nowhere. He's tried to talk to me every time I've come in, but good old me, I can do feisty when it's called for just as well as the next person.

Ignore.

Ignore.

Ignore.

The word plays in my mind on an invisible loop as I make it a point not to engage him in any type of conversation. I don't even know where he comes from or what he wants. This can't simply be about apologizing. He came out of nowhere, and now he is everywhere. Wait, is this guy actually stalking me???

Today I've walked in and marched straight to the counter, holding my hand up to hold him back when he starts to get out of his seat and approach me. My face must tell him everything he needs to know, because he plops down in his chair without a word and I take my seat at the counter, where Martin is already setting my coffee down.

"Is he still looking this way?" I whisper to Martin, moving in so no one can hear me.

Martin smirks and shakes his head at me. I know he secretly likes my kind of crazy. Maybe in another lifetime.

"He's not going anywhere," he tells me, looking over my shoulder.

"What does he want?" I ask, a sense of urgency in my voice.

"Why don't you just ask him?"

I swivel in my stool until I'm facing the stranger across the coffee shop. I cross one leg over another, my skirt riding higher, making him squirm in his seat. I want something from him and I mean to get it. Today. I want to be done with this anxiety riddling my body every time I see him and remember that I looked like a soaked beached whale carrying myself out of the coffee shop a few days ago.

I watch him as he watches me. If

I were in the market for a new man, he's exactly the kind of man I'd jump on. Actually, I'd probably jump his bones, but that's neither here nor there. I'm not yet over Tatum, and this guy is an arrogant prick, so I think I'll give him a miss. But that doesn't mean I can't very well admire the chisel of his cheeks, the golden-brown ringlets and the emerald green eyes set against his golden skin. He's handsome in an olde worlde charm sort of way, his rakish good looks knotting my insides.

I pick up my cup and stroll to his table. He looks up in surprise before his eyes fall to the empty chair, offering me a seat.

"Tell me what it is you want," I say, asking bluntly as I take a seat.

He regards me for a long moment, as though measuring his words. Anything he's said so far has made me want to kill him, so I can only imagine he doesn't want to continue down that path.

"I've been away for a few months and just got back to town. Didn't think my first accomplishment upon my return would be running into a woman and spilling coffee down her front. Not a good way to settle back in."

"And?" I ask. That still didn't tell me what he wanted.

"And nothing. I just wanted to make sure we're good."

"We're good," I tell him. "My clothes are good. My phone survived. And my ego is intact. So we're good."

"Can I get you a coffee?"

That sounded suspiciously like he meant a date. I hold up my cup to him to remind him that I already have a cup.

"Another?"

This man will stop at nothing.

"No." I'm defiant. Ruthless. "Look, thank you for your concern, but there's no need for you to be in here day in day out waiting for me to show up."

"So you'll give me your number?" he asks, an earnest look on his face. I can't help but laugh at that. The way he asked reminded me of an eager schoolboy asking a girl out for the first time. Ever.

"Not on your life, buster."

He puts a hand to his wounded chest and fixes me with a mock hurt expression, and my internal angel can't help but warm to him. I tamp her down. Literally press a firm hand on her head and tell her to get back inside her box. There's no way I want to absolve him of the guilt he feels, or at the very least, let him off the hook.

"Look, I appreciate you feeling bad about what happened, really. But there's no need for you to keep coming back here daily trying to apologize."

"The coffee here is good, too," he tells me, giving me a quirky smile. I raise my eyes in surprise that he's even had time to notice for all the stalking he's done.

"That, it is."

"Do you come here often?"

I see what he's doing and I cock my head in answer. He's trying to engage me in conversation, and if I keep staring into his gorgeous greens, I'll be swept away and there'll be no coming back for me.

And that voice. Heavens to Murgatroyd, that voice is like decadent honey flowing sensuously across my skin.

"I really have to get back to work," I say, grabbing my cup as I rise from my chair. He stops me with a hand against my own as I go to pick up my phone, and I freeze, mid-way out of my seat. A fiery electric spark zaps through my veins when his skin meets mine, and I look down at that place where our hands are comfortable with one another. That touch is like lightning and thunder, and it paralyzes me. It leaves me speechless. Because I've never felt that much energy swimming between me and another person, and it scares me. I'm absolutely terrified of the unknown.

"One drink," he says. "Just one drink. Then I'll be gone and you'll never hear from me again."

Read the full book here: https://a.co/d/0EEuUfg

Thank you so much for reading

WHEN YOU ARE MINE.
Please consider leaving an honest review for this book to help me reach more readers; https://a.co/d/gjpSgl2

Subscribe to my newsletter for FREE content and giveaways, and be the first to know about upcoming releases. Grab your FREE COPY of my novella WHITE KNIGHT here:
https://dl.bookfunnel.com/xmej6jydsa

Follow me on Facebook:
https://www.facebook.com/profile.php?id=100093985934744
EARLY ACCESS ZONES:
Join me for early access to upcoming releases pre-launch.
PATREON: patreon.com/IrisTCannon
REAM: https://reamstories.com/iriscannon

ALSO BY THE AUTHOR

ALWAYS MINE
A series of obsessive dark romance books where the characters overlap between books. Books are standalone and can be read in any order
Book 1: When You Are Mine
Book 2: Never Tear Us Apart
Book 3: At Last

DAGGER & THRONE
A three book romantasy series which must be read in order
Book 1: Queen Of My Heart
Book 2: King Of My Soul
Book 3: Heir To The Throne

SINNERS OF SEATTLE (COMING IN 2024)